Journey of the Heart

the story of Janet McLean

Jeannie M. Castleberry

Castleberry Farms Press

This is a work of fiction. All the characters and events portrayed in this book are fictitious, and any resemblance to real people or events is purely coincidental.

All scripture references are from the King James Version of the Bible.

First Edition

ISBN 1-891907-15-8

Castleberry Farms Press
P.O. Box 337
Poplar, WI 54864

Printed in the U.S.A.

Dedication

To my King, my hope and trust,

the One who loves me and fulfils every need.

You are my life.

To my sisters, Katie and Betsy Castleberry

And to my sisters in Christ,

Anna and Sarah DiPuma,

Edith Weikert, and Anna Woloszyn

From the Author

"You should write more courtship books." That was the subject of many letters my parents received, and some added, "We want to know what happened to Janet McLean." My parents considered writing more courtship books, but many questions arose. Were they becoming a substitute for romance novels? Did girls need more encouragement to wait for God's plan to unfold, or would an abundance of books make the waiting harder? We weren't sure.

God has laid a burden on my heart for young women, and my prayer is that this book will be a blessing to those who read it, encouraging them to live completely surrendered to the Lord. "Journey of the Heart" is different from most courtship books, but the storyline is based on fact, some of it from my own life. My dad is my spiritual leader and an elder in our church, and it was with his blessing and approval that the "sermon" – based on his teaching – was included.

I also wanted to bless my parents through this project. The story of my heart's journey would be far different was it not for their patient teaching, listening ears, and gentle guidance through the past few years. Mom and Dad, you have been the instrument of the Lord in my maturing and spiritual growth. Thank you for all the late-night talks, the ardent prayers, the practical advice. I love you both so much!

Lastly, but most important, this is Your book, Lord. From the very first, I knew You had called me to write it. Thank You for giving me the privilege of writing for You. You gave me the original inspiration for this project, then supplied the grace to complete it. All glory and praise goes to You!

Jeannie Castleberry 2005

Chapter One

Dawn came to southern Michigan.

It began slowly, the stars fading as the sky changed from coal to dove gray. A faint rose line etched the eastern horizon as birds began to stir, and a breeze ruffled the leaves of the apple tree. The pink line stretched higher, shades of yellow and orange beginning to appear. High on the branch of the old hollow oak in the pasture an owl blinked sleepily, shook his feathers, and dived into his hole. The light grew, spreading streaks of gold across the sky. Somewhere a robin paused in his search for a worm to greet the morning. The sun, a vermillion sphere, climbed over the dark line of firs. A new day had begun.

No one stirred on the farm, for it was still very early. The sun's rays intensified, but it was an hour before Janet McLean turned over drowsily. She yawned and sat up, trying not to wake her sisters. They were still the "little girls" to her, although Rachel was thirteen and Becky was eleven. Soon it would be time for everyone else to get up, but Janet wanted a few quiet moments alone. Dressing as noiselessly as possible, she made her way downstairs.

The colors of the sunrise were gone, but the sky was a brilliant blue. For a long moment she drank in the beauty of the morning, then turned away and pulled her Bible off the shelf. After years of sporadic attempts to become consistent in daily reading of the scriptures, Janet had found that reading first thing every morning was the only way she could make sure she would remember. Sometimes she felt nourished by what she read, and other times she wasn't sure if she got anything at all, but she knew that God would bless her efforts. This morning she read the second chapter of Philippians, and verse thirteen stood out to her: "For it is God which worketh in you both to will and to do of his good pleasure."

I do want to do Your good pleasure, Lord, she prayed silently. *Please show me how to live for Your glory.* From the sound of the footsteps overhead, Janet knew the whole family would soon be astir. She sighed softly. *Lord, help me today. I have so much to do.* Returning her Bible to its place, she headed to the basement for the milk pails. Even in bitterly cold weather Janet loved taking care of the family's dairy goats, but on a June morning like this one she couldn't imagine a better way to begin her day.

The barn door creaked open, and the goats immediately began their chorus of bleats. Bright eyes and soft noses showed over the rough boards of the pen as Janet laughed and returned the incessant greetings.

"Good morning, girls!" she called, ducking as a barn swallow whisked overhead. "How's my Nutmeg this morning?" she added, greeting the queen of the herd. The old goat got stiffly to her feet, stretched, then followed Janet out of the pen and up to the milking stand, patiently chewing her cud as her hoof was examined. Janet straightened up with a triumphant smile. "Still a little stiff, but I believe we've whipped that infection, old girl," she asserted, giving her an affectionate pat. Then she grinned sheepishly. There stood two of her brothers, who had come out to do their own chores.

"Do you think she understands what you're talking about?" Steve prodded. At sixteen, he was always finding ways to make his family laugh. "How's the spice cabinet today?"

Janet joined in the laugh. She had named the goats after spices according to their colors. Currently Nutmeg, Cinnamon, and Ginger were milking, and Steve insisted he could taste those spices in the milk. "Nice and spicy," she returned.

Steve chuckled. "I'll start the water for the heifers," he told his eighteen and a half year-old brother.

"Go ahead," Ben replied. "I'll get the mineral block and be right out." He paused to smile at his sister. "You're a good shepherdess, Janet. Thanks for taking care of the goats." Then the boys were gone.

As Janet milked, her thoughts were on the day ahead. The night before, Dad had mentioned moving the yearling steers to the north pasture, and the fence would have to be checked before that was done. The McLeans made their living raising beef cattle, and enjoyed working together. The boys did much of the work, but there were many times that Janet's help was needed as well, especially since her oldest brother was no longer living at home. Jeff, at twenty-five, had married Jenny Barker two months ago, and was busy working on his own farm a few miles away. He was glad to come and help if there was a big job, but the burden of daily chores fell on those still at home.

The warm smell of fresh muffins met Janet at the kitchen door. Rachel, wearing a floury apron, informed her that breakfast was ready. "Do you know if the boys are about through with their chores?" she questioned.

"I think so," Janet replied. "Maybe Samuel can get them," she added, as she caught a glimpse of tousled hair and a freckled face. The seven-year-old didn't wait for her to finish, but dashed out the door. Rachel and Janet laughed. It was a good morning.

As she had expected, it was a busy day. The fence was checked, the steers were moved, bread was baked, and more lettuce was planted. Janet was washing the lunch dishes when the telephone rang.

"Can I get it?" Becky asked hopefully. Janet shrugged, and Becky took that as permission. Suddenly Janet felt irritated. *Why didn't I just get it?* she asked herself as she listened to Becky.

"Hello," she was saying. "Who are you? . . . What? Oh. Well, I'll see if Janet wants to talk to you." Putting her hand over the receiver, she said loudly, "Janet, it's Stephanie Kemp. Do you want to talk to her?"

Janet rolled her eyes. "Becky!" she hissed, frowning. "She'll hear you!" Wiping her hands on a towel, she took the phone from her sister. "Hello, Stephanie! How are you?"

The voice on the other end sounded emotional. "Hi, Janet. I'm okay, I guess."

"What's going on? You don't sound like you're okay." Janet was warm and sympathetic.

"Oh, it's just things with Micah," Stephanie sighed. "Courtship certainly isn't all roses. We're having some disagreements and I'm worried that maybe things won't work out! Janet, we've been courting for five months now and if we end up breaking it off . . ." Her voice faded away. Janet found herself groping for words.

"It will be okay, Stephanie," she began. "God has a plan for your life, and He has one for Micah, too. I know you're in a hard situation and it's difficult to see how it will all work out." She didn't know if she was comforting her friend or not, but she wanted to help. "Are these major disagreements? I mean, can you work them out?"

"Oh, probably. His family just does some things differently than mine does, and it would be hard to get used to it! For example, his dad sets up the homeschooling curriculum and schedule, and his mom does the teaching. My mom has always planned the school year in our family. Wouldn't it be hard to teach using someone else's plans?"

"Maybe, but I can actually see some advantages," Janet answered. "If your children argued about a subject, you could say, 'Talk to Dad!' Besides, isn't that the way regular schools do it?"

Stephanie laughed. "That's almost exactly what Micah said. I guess I would get used to it, but it sure sounds different. Another thing is cars. I don't know anything about car care besides filling up with gas. And he wants me to learn to check oil and belts and fluids and I don't know what all! Starting out in law enforcement, he has a lot of unpredictable shifts, and he said it would help him if I could do that."

"We're in the same boat on that one!" Janet exclaimed. "I've heard all about my 'mechanical abilities,' or lack thereof, for years."

As the conversation continued, Janet realized that Stephanie's problems were not major ones, and certainly possible to solve. In fact, the process of working them out would help her relationship with Micah to grow deeper. It sounded like Stephanie was having an emotional day, and had let her problems grow out of proportion, making them look worse than they really were.

"Well, thanks for listening," she was saying. "It sure helps to talk to you and know that you care! Thank you for praying, too. I really need it!"

"I'm glad I can pray for you," Janet replied. "I just wish you lived closer so we could see each other!"

Stephanie laughed. "Any time you feel like coming to Arkansas, you just go ahead!" The girls had met twice, once at a homeschool convention, and once when Stephanie had a wedding to attend a few hours away. However, they had been pen pals for years, and had a close friendship despite the geographical distance.

"Well, I should probably let you go," Stephanie said.

"I should probably finish the dishes!" Janet answered. "Thanks for calling . . . and Stephanie, don't worry. God has everything planned."

As Janet turned her attention back to the kitchen, she saw that Becky had finished drying all the clean dishes and had put most of them away. She had also wiped the table and swept the floor. What a hard worker she was, and so good natured. What did it matter if she wasn't very gracious on the phone? That would come with time and practice.

"You should apologize for the way you acted," Janet's conscience whispered.

Oh, it probably didn't bother her, she argued.

"If it didn't, that means you do it a lot."

Well, she ought to know how to be polite! After all, she is eleven!

"And you ought to know how to be polite to her. You're twenty-two."

Janet cleared her throat. She felt her face turn red. Then she started washing the dishes again. *I'll apologize in a little while,* she told herself. *I don't know exactly how to say it.*

"Just say, 'I'm sorry, Becky,'" her conscience prompted. Janet knew the longer she waited, the harder it would become, but still she hesitated. Two forces were wrestling for control, and suddenly she thought, *I'm resisting the Holy Spirit.*

"I'm sorry, Becky," she began. Her voice sounded hollow, and to her surprise, it shook. "I was rude to you."

Becky just smiled. "That's okay," she responded. "I don't mind."

Her answer cut Janet to the heart. Was it possible that she had been unkind to Becky so often that it no longer bothered her? "Becky," she added, "I'm rude to you a lot. I'm sorry." It was hard to say, but the relief was immediate.

"That's okay," Becky said again.

Dishes finished, Janet turned to the other tasks for the afternoon, glad that she would have some time alone. She needed to do some deep thinking.

Chapter Two

The iron moved slowly over the green and white tablecloth. Janet hummed softly, but her mind wasn't on the song. Her thoughts were a jumble of Stephanie, Becky, and her married sister Sarah. Especially Sarah. Janet still missed her, although after six years it no longer seemed strange that she was a married woman. She smiled, remembering the first time Sarah visited with her baby, Judah. Janet had found it difficult to realize that Judah was her nephew, not a new brother. Now she was "Aunt Janet" to Judah and Noah, and simply "Danny" to little Lydia. Sarah's fourth child was due in late November.

Yes, God had blessed Sarah, Janet reflected with a twinge of envy. Becoming Mrs. Luke Williams at twenty-one, she was a mother a year later – *the same age I am now.* Janet sighed. *I want to get married so much! Why isn't there anyone for me? Maybe I'm not mature enough,* she thought, remembering the situation with Becky an hour ago. *I do get irritated sometimes. But no one is perfect. Sarah wasn't, Jenny wasn't, Stephanie isn't. And God gave all of them someone.* She recalled Jeff and Jenny's courtship. She and Jenny had been friends for years, and had become very close during the time before the wedding two months ago. "I used to wonder if I would ever get married," Jenny had confided. "It seemed like such a long time to wait."

Janet sighed again. Jenny and Stephanie were both two years younger than she was, and both of them were already courting or married. *They thought they had to wait a long time,* she grumbled mentally. *I've already waited two years longer, and there are still no prospects.* She turned off the iron and brushed back a strand of hair. *What am I doing wrong? Why hasn't God given me someone?*

"Janet?" Rachel's voice broke into her thoughts. "Becky and I were wondering if you want to take a walk with us. We were going to look for wild strawberries."

Janet smiled in spite of herself. "That sounds like fun. Sure, let's go."

Rachel and Becky walked ahead of her, talking and laughing. They had so much fun together. Janet felt a little sorry for herself. Why couldn't she have a close friend? She and Sarah hadn't been as close as the younger girls, and while Janet's relationship with Mom had improved greatly over the past few years, she still didn't feel the close companionship she desired. She knew she was loved tremendously, yet so often she felt alone and misunderstood. Her sister-in-law Jenny was wonderful, but completely wrapped up in her new married life. *Which is how it should be*, Janet admitted. That left Stephanie, her closest friend. If only she lived closer.

"I found one!" Becky's excited cry brought Janet out of her reflections with a start. *That's right, we're looking for strawberries,* she remembered. Glancing down, she saw a gleam of red almost under her feet, then another.

"Oh, girls, they're everywhere!" she exclaimed. She knelt to sample one. The tiny, slightly tart fruits always made her think of pioneers, for some reason. Smiling, she thought how tame her life would seem to them. Where there had once been only forests, there were fenced pastures, level hayfields, sturdy houses and barns, and good roads. The woods that she found so thrilling would have seemed like a back yard to them.

"We forgot a basket," eleven-year-old Becky giggled. "I guess we'll have to eat everything we pick."

Janet laughed, too. "I hope we don't get stomach aches," she smiled, looking at the handful of berries Rachel held. "We'll probably get about ten strawberries apiece."

The girls sat in the short grass, enjoying the sunshine and the berries. *There's no excuse for being moody on such a pretty day,* Janet told herself, determined to join the fun.

"Doesn't this seem old-fashioned?" Rachel was asking. "I feel like a pioneer!"

"I was just thinking the same thing," Janet agreed.

"I'm thinking it now, too," Becky chimed in. Her eyes sparkled. "Janet, wouldn't it be fun to have a picnic out here? Just us girls?"

Janet started to answer, "I'm too busy," but caught herself just in time. If she always turned down the girls' invitations, no wonder she felt left out! And Becky's "just us girls," while rather ungrammatical, had a warm ring to it. Maybe they did consider her to be one of them.

"Yes, let's do it," she agreed, with such enthusiasm that Rachel glanced at her, surprised. Janet blushed, but continued to warm to the idea. "Let's make it a pioneer picnic. We can all wear sunbonnets and carry a quilt to sit on."

The girls planned the picnic all the way home, snatches of the conversation continuing throughout the evening. Caught up in planning, Janet forgot her earlier frustrations, and the end of the day found her in a pleasant frame of mind. "Tomorrow I should write Stephanie and encourage her to think of something besides her problems," Janet said half-aloud as she washed the milk pails. "She needs to think more about others."

Four days passed before Janet found time to write, however. It seemed there were a thousand things clamoring for her attention, and all truly needed doing. On Friday afternoon, the picnic over, Janet pulled out a piece of paper and rummaged through the drawer for a pen. She had a little time while the bread baked.

She wrote slowly at first, trying to organize her thoughts, then gathered momentum as she wrote line after line.

"It was good to talk to you . . . I wish there was some way I could help you . . . Give your burden to the Lord . . . These are growing times for you and Micah. Remember how we used to imagine our futures? I guess we forgot there would be trials in courtship, too! But everyone is human, and we live in a fallen world . . . Don't give up. God is doing something great in your life . . . Try to keep your thoughts on Him (although you have to think about Micah, too, I know!) and on serving others . . . I love you and pray for you daily! Please keep me posted . . . Love, Janet."

She was still in a writing mood when she finished the letter, so she ran upstairs for her journal. The smell of baking bread wafted through the kitchen.

June 9

I just wrote Stephanie. Sigh. She's having a rough time, poor girl. She called earlier this week to tell me her courtship troubles, and I tried to encourage her. But I find it hard to understand what the big struggle is. I mean, she's courting, isn't she? How hard can it be? I wish she could be in my place for a while – single as an odd sock! She has no idea what it's like to sit here and <u>*wait*</u> *(for an indefinite length of time!) for someone like Micah to show up.*

But I really am glad she shares her struggles with me. It's good to feel needed, and to feel that I'm actually able to encourage her. I'm also glad that she trusts me enough to open up and tell me how she's really doing.

Well, I think my bread is done, so I should put this away. I hope that God will send me a husband – or at least a possibility! – soon. (Please, Lord!) But if I have to wait, I guess there are some lessons to be learned now, too.

Janet enjoyed the silent listening ear her journal offered. Starting the "diary habit," as Steve called it, at age fourteen, her journals were a hodgepodge record of daily life, dreams for the future, and thoughts on nearly every subject. The earlier journals were amusing to read through, seeing the world again through the immature eyes of early teens, but growth was evident as time passed. Janet's journals had begun recording more and more of her spiritual life.

Now, as she buttered the tops of the crusty loaves, she frowned over the last line of her most recent entry. What lessons were there to learn, besides patience?

Chapter Three

The weeks slipped past. Janet realized one day, with some surprise, that it was mid-July. Where had the time gone? With all the farm work, summer had a way of disappearing. The McLeans were already making their second crop of hay, and Janet was taking a turn raking with the smaller tractor, while Ben mowed the north field. Dad and Steve were occupied with the baler. Some obscure problem with the knotter had resulted in hours of labor and dozens of parts scattered across the shop floor. Janet shook her head, thankful that getting the ancient machine back in running condition wasn't her responsibility.

No, she much preferred using the clattering old hay rake, watching the long swaths being swept into smooth, even windrows. A flock of seagulls from Lake Michigan swirled above her, their small eyes searching for mice and grasshoppers. *How do they always know when we're making hay?* she wondered. Shading her eyes, she looked at the north field. Sure enough, a few gulls were circling Ben, who looked like a speck of blue on a toy tractor.

An unfamiliar sound made her turn sharply and step on the clutch. Her quick reaction probably saved Steve a lot of work, for the rake had picked up a long piece of fence wire, and having woven it through the tines, was on the verge of hiding it among the gears and belts. Shutting off the tractor, Janet jumped down and tried to untangle the wire, but without much result. "I guess this requires wire cutters," she muttered under her breath.

"Do you want me to come help?" Steve offered hopefully when he heard the story. He cast a meaningful glance at the mess on the shop floor.

"Thanks," Janet replied, "but it's not bad. I think I can handle it. Besides," she continued, her eyes twinkling, "looks like Dad sort of needs you here." At Steve's crestfallen look, she added, "When you're done here, you can take over the raking."

Steve grinned in return. "I'll have a surprise for you when I come out."

"A surprise?" Janet echoed. "Like what?"

"Okay, you two," Dad broke in with a chuckle. "Let's get back to work. We'll be through here in about fifteen minutes, and I was hoping to start baling around one o' clock."

Janet checked her watch. "It's eleven-thirty now. I'd better hurry."

The wire was easy to remove with the proper tools, and soon the little tractor was on its way again. The sun was warm on Janet's back. Her eyes and hands were busy, but her mind was free to think. For some reason, she always felt like singing while raking. The song that came to mind was one of her favorites.

"To God be the glory – great things He hath done! So loved He the world that He gave us His Son, Who yielded His life an atonement for sin, And opened the life-gate that all may go in.

"Praise the Lord, praise the Lord, let the earth hear His voice! Praise the Lord, praise the Lord, let the people rejoice! Oh, come to the Father through Jesus the Son, And give Him the glory – great things He hath done!"

As she ended the ninth round, Steve appeared carrying a gas can. He motioned for her to turn off the tractor, then came rustling through the hay to fill the tank.

"Is that the surprise?" Janet grinned.

"No, but you were about to get an unpleasant one!" he returned. "You're almost out of gas. Let's see . . . it was probably just about enough to get you to the far end of the field."

"Thanks, Steve. I'm glad you thought of it! But I'm curious – what's the surprise?"

Steve didn't answer for a moment, concentrating on the task at hand. He removed the gas can spout and carefully screwed the cap back on. Janet was ready to ask him again when he began to sing.

"On a bright and sunny morn,
Ben went out to hoe the corn.
He must have thought it went too slow,
He took an axe and not a hoe.
Ben killed a snake between the rows,
Before he saw it was just a hose.
Rachel likes to bake and cook,
She really ought to use a book.
Her meals can be somewhat unique,
At recipes she hates to peek.
Maybe it seems a little silly

But I don't like cinnamon in my chili!"

"Where did you come up with that?" Janet asked, laughing.

Steve tapped his head wisely. "I have many interesting things in here," he assured her solemnly. "I'm writing one about you next."

"Oh, no," she groaned in mock horror. "Please say it's not about the wire in the rake!"

"Oh, yes," he answered, "and several other mishaps, as well. In fact, it may take more than one verse! Everyone will enjoy it." He handed her the empty gas can. "Now run along and eat lunch before we start baling. I've already had mine."

Still laughing, Janet turned toward the house. Steve was so much fun. Over the past few weeks, she had increasingly realized how much she loved and enjoyed her family. They always liked working together, but there was something special about the way everyone pulled together at haying time, racing against threatening thunderstorms, dealing with broken machinery, and enduring long days of dust and heat.

Janet was at her best when faced with a challenge. Her nature thrived on hard work, and as Steve put it, "Janet without ideas is like the Sahara Desert without sand." She loved finding the best ways to do things, often borrowing ideas from other families and adapting them to fit her family's needs. When she was younger, she had found it difficult to accept her parents' methods, causing much tension with her constant criticisms, but the Lord had helped her mature. Now she sought to serve her family, especially her parents, with her talents and hardworking attitude.

"Hi," Rachel greeted Janet as she stood in the entryway, trying to let her eyes adjust to the relative darkness of the house. "We've got a sandwich ready for you, Janet. Dad and Samuel just went out to check the hay, so you'd better eat."

"Yes, Dad wanted to start baling soon," Becky added. "I think Mom is going to do the dishes while we help outside." Her eyes danced. "Dad said I could ride the rack with you today."

Janet returned Becky's smile. "That's hard work," she warned, "but it will be fun." Becky could drag hay bales to the back of the wagon, and Janet would stack them. *It seems like only last year that I was dragging bales for Jeff.* The years had a way of marching on.

After a quick lunch, the girls returned to the field. Samuel stood watching Dad grease the baler, his hands thrust deep into his pockets. With his cap on the back of his head, he seriously contemplated the workings of the machine, slowly chewing on a piece of hay. Becky couldn't repress a giggle.

"What is it?" Rachel whispered.

"His shoes," Becky whispered back. "Look at what he's wearing!"

Both girls followed her pointing finger. He had worn house slippers to the field, and now stood in a classic farmer pose, oblivious to the girls as well as his unusual footwear.

Dad straightened up. "Looks like we're ready," he announced. "Got your gloves, Becky?" Then he, too, noticed Samuel's feet. "Son," he chuckled, "I can tell you are as comfortable in the hayfield as you are in the living room. That's a good thing when you're a farmer. But you might need some better protection for your feet today."

Samuel looked down. "Why, how . . . they're not even mine!" He began to laugh. "These are Steve's house slippers." He took off running for the house, shuffling to keep the too-big slippers on his feet.

"Here come Steve and Ben now," Janet said.

"Where's Samuel going in such a hurry?" Ben queried, watching the retreating figure. Both boys had to laugh when they heard the story. When Samuel reappeared, the irrepressible Steve had already started a new verse for his song. As Janet and Becky climbed onto the hay wagon, they heard Samuel's giggle as Steve sang, "Living room or hayfield, Samuel's feet are warm. He wears his brother's slippers, to keep his own from harm."

The tractor started with a sputter and a puff of black exhaust. The wagon jerked and swayed, following the baler's convulsive movements as it gobbled the windrows, compressing the hay into tight bales, tying them with ropes, then spitting them onto the chute that led to the wagon. At first the work was easy, Becky dragging the bales to the back of the wagon and Janet stacking them in careful patterns. Standing and walking on the jolting floor was challenging for Becky at first, but when Janet showed her how to keep her knees flexed, she soon caught on.

Gradually the wagon filled, the tipsy load bouncing as it traveled over ruts and bumps. Janet motioned for Becky to go up and ride on the top. "It's getting crowded down here," she shouted over the racket made by the baler. Becky nodded and clambered up, leaving Janet to race against the machine. The hay dust was thick this close to the machine, and Janet felt parched and short of breath. Determinedly she swung yet another bale into place, undaunted by the sight of blood on her arms. The sharp hay stems left dozens of tiny cuts, but that was to be expected.

Wiping her forehead and taking a deep breath, she bent to grab the next bale in the never-ending stream, but something was wrong. This bale had only one rope instead of two, and would fall apart as soon as it left the chute. She straightened up and waved for Dad to stop.

"Looks like you've got a full load," he commented, carrying the broken bale around to the front of the machine where it could be baled again. "I think we'll head back and I'll check the knotter."

With a sigh of relief, Janet headed to the top of the load. She sank down gratefully beside Becky. "Warm out here, isn't it?" she smiled. "How did you like your first time on the wagon?"

Becky's face was flushed, but her eyes still sparkled. "It was fun. Rachel and I are going to unload this one while Ben goes out."

That means Steve and I will stack in the hayloft, Janet thought. The sun was hot out in the field, but at least there was a breeze. The loft, with its metal roof, would be sweltering.

Sure enough, the hayloft felt like an oven. Waves of heat rose shimmering off the floor to hang in the air along with clouds of dust. The elevator screeched and groaned as it carried the bales almost four stories high, depositing them on a long ramp that sent them sliding nearly to the far end of the loft. Trickles of sweat left trails in the dust on Janet's face, and stung her eyes as she bent to pick up another bale. They were stacking six bales high, but she could only manage four layers. Even then, Steve was far faster. He threw the bales to the upper layers, grinning at Janet's disheveled appearance, and she scrambled up to stack them properly.

Just when she felt almost overcome by the heat and dust, the elevator stopped abruptly. The last bale, loud in the sudden quiet, slid down the ramp and landed with a muffled thud at the bottom. Steve swung it into place as Janet slipped off the stack, arms and legs trembling a little from the frantic pace.

"Whew," she breathed. "Let's go get some water."

"Sounds good to me," Steve returned heartily.

Load followed load, everyone rotating jobs as the hay was baled, hauled in, and stacked. Janet was amazed to find that it was already seven o'clock when they finished baling and stopped for supper. Only one hay wagon sat waiting to be unloaded.

"Rachel and Becky, why don't you help Mom with the dishes and whatever else she needs, and Janet can do the milking," Dad suggested. "Ben, Steve, and I can finish what's left of the hay, then we'll do chores." He smiled at Samuel. "You can help me give the yearling heifers some new pasture. I know you've helped Mom a lot today, and we all appreciate that."

Samuel beamed. Sometimes he found it hard to be the youngest and not able to do everything his older siblings did. He loved helping Dad with a 'grown-up' job, especially anything that concerned the beef cattle.

Janet tried to milk quickly that night, but her hands were blistered and sore. *It's been a good day,* she reflected. *Eight hundred bales of hay, and no injuries.* Tired as she was, her heart overflowed with thanksgiving for God's goodness.

Chapter Four

"Janet, can we talk while you sew?" Mom asked one afternoon. It was a warm day in late August, and crickets chirped a lazy farewell to summer under the open living room window.

"Sure," she replied, pulling the nearly finished skirt onto her lap so Mom could share the couch. "This hem will take awhile."

Mom sat down and looked out the window for a long moment before beginning. Janet, feeling uncomfortable, started trying to remember the last few days. *Have I done something wrong?* she wondered, feeling fidgety. Nothing came to mind, however.

"I'm sorry, Janet." Mom seemed to realize that Janet was wondering what was going on. "I'm just trying to figure out how to start."

Just say it, Janet felt like wailing. She would much rather know what the problem was than wonder about it. *Just tell me and get it over with!* But aloud she said nothing, waiting for Mom to collect her thoughts.

"It's about this fall," Mom said finally, focusing her attention on her daughter. "Dad and I have been talking, and we want you to help with the homeschooling."

Janet smiled with relief. "I thought something was wrong! I've been helping with school since I graduated, so that shouldn't be a problem."

"Yes, you have been helping, and I really appreciate all the help you've given me over the years. But this year will be different. Instead of just asking you to check a math lesson occasionally or give a spelling test, we want you to have more responsibility."

"What do you mean?"

"Well, we want you to be sort of an assistant teacher. You'll have some classes that you are responsible for – planning lessons, teaching, giving assignments, and correcting papers."

Janet took a deep breath. "I don't know if I can do that! I've never . . . I mean, how do you teach? I've never tried . . . I don't know how . . ." Her voice trailed off.

Mom smiled. "There's a first time for everything. I'll help you, of course. And I'm sure you can handle it. You've always been good at taking hold of a problem and figuring out how to solve it."

Janet was silent, trying to understand the scope of this new challenge. Could she do it? *I'm sure God will give me the grace,* she thought. *But it will be tough.* At least it wasn't time to start yet. She knotted the thread and snipped the end.

"Dad and I feel this will be a good experience for you," Mom was saying. "It will also help me a lot. Samuel needs quite a bit of one-on-one time this year, and I'll be busy with that. Steve still has two years to go, and the girls have several subjects that need real teaching this year – it's a lot for me to do alone."

Janet didn't even consider arguing. It sounded like it was already settled, and she would accept her parents' decision, although she was not without apprehension. "Okay, Mom," she said, smiling bravely. "You'll have to teach me how to teach!"

"Good! Thank you for being so willing. Perhaps we should go ahead and discuss classes, since school starts in three weeks."

The scissors dropped to the floor with a clatter. "Three weeks! Why, that's not enough time! I can't possibly be ready!"

"Yes, you can," Mom soothed. "Let's go to the schoolroom and look things over."

Forty-five minutes later, Janet headed outside for a quick walk before supper. Her head was spinning. There was much more involved than she had expected. *How am I going to do this? Teach math to Rachel and Becky? I've never been good at math myself – how can I teach them? And history . . . at least I enjoy that, but how do you* <u>*teach*</u> *it?* Dropping on a bench in the woods, she buried her face in her hands.

"God, please help me," she prayed aloud. "This looks too hard for me. How can I do it, Lord? How?" Too confused to form a coherent prayer, she kept repeating, "Help me – I need Your strength. I need Your wisdom." A sparrow hopped out of the underbrush near her feet, but she barely noticed it. All her thoughts were consumed by this unexpected change in her life.

After a time she rose and continued her walk. It was a beautiful day, but it could have been snowing for all she knew. One thought pulsed relentlessly through her mind: *I'm going to teach and I don't know how.* It was different from most tasks she had tackled without hesitation. She felt the responsibility keenly. If she didn't do a good job, she would be cheating Rachel and Becky out of a good education. What if she accidently taught them something wrong in math and they had to relearn it? Everything would be her fault. And her parents were trusting her to do it right. "Dear Lord," she said again, "I can't do it. Help me!"

"You can't hear God if you're always talking." Her pastor's words came to her with sudden clarity, and she realized that she had been so busy crying out for help that she hadn't even thought about God's replies. Now she tried to remember promises from scripture, but only broken phrases found their way into her muddled thoughts. *"Peace I leave with you, my peace I give unto you . . . Wait on the Lord, be of good courage . . . I will never leave thee . . . If any man lack wisdom, let him ask of God."* Even the fragments of His words brought comfort. She closed her eyes, leaning against a tree. *Lord, calm my spirit. Help me to trust You. I know I won't be doing this alone.* She drew in her breath sharply as she realized that she was calling on the Lord in a way she hadn't done for a long time. Usually confident in her own abilities, she rarely felt as helpless as she did now. Brokenness before the Lord was not a common experience for Janet.

"Lord, forgive me. Humble me." Tears of repentance stung her eyes. "God, I can't do it in my own power. I can't do <u>anything</u> in my own power!" The words came from a softened heart.

That evening, Janet decided to call Stephanie and tell her about teaching. *My "big news,"* she thought. *Not what I was hoping for, but at least it's news.*

To her surprise, Stephanie didn't have much comment. "That should be interesting," she said. "I'll pray for you. I'm sure you'll do fine." Then she started talking about Micah and the latest developments in their courtship.

Janet swallowed a little prick of pain. Stephanie didn't seem too interested in her life. *But I need to be here for her,* she reminded herself. *A courtship is much more important, and a good friend is a good listener.* She pushed her own thoughts aside and focused on the things Stephanie was interested in conversing about. The phone call left her vaguely disappointed.

The time before school was to begin seemed to have wings. The last week was especially hectic, since Mom always wanted to do the fall housecleaning before diving into full-time lessons. Normally Janet enjoyed the job, but this year she wished she could work on lesson plans instead.

"You don't have to prepare for the whole year before you start," Ben reminded her.

"I know." She sighed. "I just feel so overwhelmed."

"At least Rachel and Becky aren't first graders, so you don't have to start at the very beginning. You'll do fine," he encouraged. "Mom didn't have any experience when she started, but she managed to do a great job with us." He smiled. "I'll be praying for you."

"Thanks, Ben," Janet said softly. "I appreciate that."

Sunday night found Janet in the schoolroom, going over and over the next day's lesson. *Oh, I hope I thought of everything!* she worried. *What if I forget what I was going to say? What if I don't know the answer to a question? I'm the teacher – I have to know the answers!*

The living room clock struck ten. Janet knew she should go to bed, but she was wide awake, filled with anxiety. There were bits of paper on the floor. *Might as well sweep,* she thought. *I couldn't sleep if I went to bed anyway.*

The soft swishing of the broom brought a sleepy Mom to the doorway. "Why Janet, I thought you were in bed! Why are you still up?" She looked at Janet's strained expression. "Are you nervous about tomorrow?"

Janet felt the emotion welling up. "I guess," she replied simply, not trusting her voice for more. She bent to pick up the dustpan, then turned to face Mom. Her gentle face was full of love and compassion, and Janet longed to tell her how she felt. Mom would comfort and help her. She couldn't find the words, though, so she merely went to the closet to put away the broom.

Mom started to follow her, then thought better of it. Sarah would have told her everything, but Janet was far more reserved with her feelings. It was when she wouldn't talk about something that Mom knew it affected her deeply. The best thing to do was pray for her and wait until she was ready to talk.

After brushing her teeth, Janet started upstairs. A light left on in the schoolroom caught her eye. Going in to turn it off, she glanced around the room one last time. Tomorrow . . . She turned away, but her gaze fell on the blackboard. Mom's lovely handwriting read:

Welcome to the First Day of School!
"Commit thy way unto the Lord; trust also in Him;
and He will bring it to pass."
Psalm 37:5

Janet looked at it for a long moment. Had she already forgotten to call on the Lord? Her anxious thoughts a few minutes ago had not contained a plea for help. *Lord, help me as I teach tomorrow,* she prayed silently. *And help me remember to call on You.*

Chapter Five

September 8

Well, my first day of teaching is over. What an experience! And do I have a lot to learn!

To begin with, we all sat in the living room and Mom prayed, asking God's blessing on our school year. I added a silent prayer of my own, asking for strength and wisdom. Next time I'll have to pray for a good attitude, too – more about that later.

Then we sang a couple of songs. I was so nervous I don't even remember what they were. I think maybe one was "Trust and Obey." After we were through singing, Rachel, Becky, and I went into the schoolroom (Mom and Samuel were going to work in the living room so they wouldn't disturb us). The big moment had arrived.

I had no clue how to begin a math class. So I started by doing a few practice problems on the blackboard, explaining as I went. Then I told the girls to start on their lessons. It wasn't three minutes before Becky was saying she couldn't remember how to work the problems. The more I tried to explain, the more bewildered she got, and pretty soon she was in tears (and I was close!).

Finally got her straightened out only to see Rachel staring out the window. She said she couldn't work her problems either. I was really getting frustrated by this time. Both girls had assured me they understood when I was explaining the lesson, and now they acted like they didn't know which end of the pencil to write with!

Somehow I got through the class. Somehow I survived until lunchtime. The girls were only supposed to read their history today (we'll discuss it tomorrow), so that class was easy. But I don't see how I can do this all year! How has Mom taught for so long without going nuts?

Janet capped her pen and shoved her journal into the desk drawer. She rubbed her aching forehead, not daring to think of the days and weeks and months that stretched ahead of her. A tear dropped on the desk and she whisked it away impatiently. "Don't be a baby," she told herself. "You can handle this." But she wondered.

The first two weeks of school were like a nightmare to Janet. The girls were not bad students, but they had forgotten a lot over the summer. Besides lesson planning, checking papers, and endless explanations, there was still her share of the normal housework, cooking, laundry, and dishes. She rose early each morning, and often sat up late at night preparing for the next day. Utterly consumed by the desire to do everything perfectly, she scarcely noticed the changing season. The crickets chirped incessantly, the aspens shimmered with gold, and the air had a frosty nip in the morning that hurried her on the way to milking. One morning a flock of geese flew over, the long honking V silhouetted against the pale purple of the sky. Janet stood watching for an instant, thrilled as always by their unerring path. Before they had even disappeared, however, she was hurrying on, mindful of the clock and her approaching class.

Far greater than the demands of teaching were the burdens Janet had laid on herself. She felt that her students' success or failure rested entirely on her efforts, and no one could accuse her of teaching half-heartedly. She threw herself into her task with such vigor, and with such complete disregard of her own needs, that she was on the verge of collapse after only a few weeks.

"Why don't you go out and take a walk, Janet?" Mom suggested one lovely afternoon.

"Oh, I can't," she replied absently, scribbling history questions with feverish haste.

"Yes, you can, and you should. It's not good for you to stay in all the time. And I think you are working too hard."

Janet, engrossed in her work, did not hear or look up.

"Janet." Mom's voice was firm. "Put down your pen."

Startled, she obeyed, turning to face her mother. "I'm sorry, Mom," she blushed. "I really don't even know what you said."

Mom smiled, but her eyes were troubled. "You're working too hard, dear. You're missing all this beautiful weather. Have you even been outside this week?"

"Just for milking."

"That's not good," Mom said, shaking her head. "I know you are taking teaching very seriously, and I appreciate your hard work, but Dad and I are worried about you. You don't seem like yourself. Tell me what is wrong." It was unusual for Mom to come to the point this quickly, and Janet heard real concern in her voice.

"Oh, I don't think anything is wrong," she began wearily, unconsciously pressing her hand against her throbbing temple. "I'm just a little overwhelmed with teaching, that's all. Seems like it's a full-time job!" she finished, with a little laugh.

Mom was shaking her head again. "The girls have years of school left, Janet. They don't have to learn everything this year. Homeschooling is part of life, but not all of life!"

To her surprise, Janet felt tears running down her cheeks. Mom had put her tangled thoughts into words – the idea that had tormented her all day was that there must be more to life than this endless, exhausting round.

Mom's arm was around her shoulder. "Tell me everything," she encouraged gently, and for once Janet put aside her fears of not being understood.

"I feel like I can't do a good job, no matter how hard I try," she started slowly. "And it's not that I can't please you, because you have said I'm doing a good job. But I feel like the girls aren't getting what they need, and I'm responsible for them! I don't want them to go through life crippled by my poor teaching."

"Oh, honey, I felt just like that when I started teaching!" Mom exclaimed. "You don't have to worry about that – you're doing a great job. Did you know that yesterday Becky told me she finally understands long division? She said, 'Janet just has a good way of explaining it.' And Rachel said she loves the history class and the historical fiction you find for them that goes along with what you are studying.

"And Janet," she continued, "Remember that God is in control of our lives, and He will help the girls learn what they need to serve Him. Don't put such a burden on yourself."

Janet wiped her eyes. "Thanks, Mom," she smiled weakly.

Mom smiled back. "Next time you feel overwhelmed, let me know! At least I'll be able to pray for you. Now go out and enjoy the afternoon."

The woods were peaceful and refreshing. The breeze cooled Janet's hot face, the quiet soothed her aching head, and the exercise stirred her blood and gave her new energy. *I should do this every day,* she thought. In the midst of all the peace and beauty, however, she felt vaguely uneasy, as if she was forgetting or neglecting something important. It seemed like it had to do with something Mom had said, something about God being in control . . . "Don't put such a burden on yourself."

That was it. Somehow she'd been doing it wrong, trying to shoulder her task in her own strength. *Well, I've never run from a challenge before. But maybe I'm not as strong as I think. Maybe I'm trying to carry something I should leave with God.* She had to teach, though. How could she let the Lord carry her burden? Maybe it had to do with trusting Him with the outcome of her efforts. She turned back toward the house. A bit of scripture flitted through her mind, the one about Jesus' yoke being "easy"– why could she never remember whole passages? Her steps quickened. She would go look up the verse.

"Come unto me, all ye that labor and are heavy laden, and I will give you rest. Take my yoke upon you, and learn of me; for I am meek and lowly in heart: and ye shall find rest unto your souls. For my yoke is easy, and my burden is light" (Matthew 11:28-30).

It hadn't taken much hunting to find the passage, and sure enough, it fitted perfectly. A deep peace stole over her, and she closed her eyes. "Thank You for this gift, Father," she whispered. "Thank You for making Your word so alive and real. And thank You for this burden, for with Your strength it is light. Let me learn of You how to bear it."

That day marked a change in Janet's teaching. Still diligent and conscientious, she was visibly more relaxed, and her stress lessened considerably. The job was still demanding, but she no longer felt everything hinged on her performance. Some One else was responsible for the girls' education, Some One far wiser than Janet.

"I'm learning more than the girls are!" she confided to Stephanie on the phone in early October. "The Lord has been so good to me. I would never have chosen to do this, but He knew it was what I needed. It has forced me to lean on Him."

"That's great, Janet," Stephanie responded warmly. "You know, I've found that God seems to give me things I can't handle so I'll keep calling on Him for grace."

"Absolutely," Janet laughed. "That's exactly what I'm learning. And a side benefit of all this is that I don't have time to feel sorry for myself about the fact that no one is courting me!"

It was true, she reflected later. She hadn't even thought of courtship since school started. *Nice to have something else to focus on,* she admitted. Still, the work was hard. Many times she felt the familiar pull to be in control, to rely on her own wisdom and abilities to get her through a difficult moment, and she succumbed more often than she would admit. Even that helped her to grow, however, for she felt rebuked of the Lord, and learned to confess and be forgiven. Slowly, gradually, Janet was being sanctified.

Chapter Six

Rrrrring . . . rrrrring . . . Janet groped for consciousness. Rrrring . . . What was that? Rrrring . . . Oh, the telephone! She stumbled across the bedroom floor and down to the kitchen, blinking as she switched on the light. *It must be the middle of the night,* she thought. *Who would be calling? Something must be wrong!*

"Hello," she said sleepily.

"Hi, is this Janet?" asked a man's voice.

"Luke! Is everything okay?"

"Just fine! We have a new baby, a little girl."

Relief flooded over her. "Praise the Lord!" she exclaimed, beaming at her parents who had appeared in the doorway. "Do you want to talk to Mom?" Handing the phone to Mom, she immediately set Dad's fears to rest. "Luke and Sarah have a new baby," she whispered, watching his face light up with joy.

Janet couldn't fall back to sleep right away. She was too excited, not only for Luke and Sarah, but also for herself. Her sister had needed a helper after Lydia's birth, and Janet spent three weeks caring for the two boys, cooking, and cleaning. Ordinary jobs were fun at someone else's house. *I'll probably never outgrow that,* she admitted, smiling in the dark. Sarah had already mentioned needing a helper when this baby was born, so Janet knew she would probably leave in the next day or two. It would be a welcome break from school.

The next morning found her up bright and early despite her lack of sleep. At the breakfast table the conversation centered around the "other McLeans," as Samuel insisted on calling Luke and Sarah's family, despite being told they were Williams. "Can we all go see the baby?" he asked hopefully.

"We'll go, but not today," Mom replied. "If Sarah wants Janet to come help, maybe we can all go along to see the baby."

If? Janet thought. Aloud she said, "Sarah already said she would need help."

"Well, she is supposed to call today, so we'll find out if that's still the plan," Mom answered calmly. "Samuel, finish your breakfast, please."

The telephone rang at about nine thirty, and Rachel and Becky raced to answer it. Both girls touched the receiver at the same time, but it did not ring again. Janet tried to repress a smile. "I think Mom answered it in the living room," she told them. The girls looked at each other, and Becky giggled.

"Do you think it's Sarah?" Rachel asked.

"Probably," Janet returned, trying to act mature. She felt like jumping up and down, but of course an adult wouldn't do that.

In a moment Mom came into the schoolroom, smiling broadly. "Sarah sounded like she feels good," she said. "They named the baby Esther Joy, and Sarah said she has a lot of brown hair."

Samuel came running in. "Can we go see her?"

Mom's eyes were soft as she looked at her youngest son. She had often wished that the Lord had sent another child so Samuel could be a big brother, for he loved babies and little children. But there was always a youngest child, and she accepted God's will. At least he could enjoy Sarah's children.

"I think we'll go tomorrow, if that's a good time for Dad," she replied.

"I guess I should pack tonight, then," Janet said.

"Well, I need to tell you about that." Mom turned to Janet. "Sarah said that she wants you to come, but she and Luke have decided that since you were there after Lydia's birth, it would be more fair for one of his sisters to have a turn. She said Anna will be going."

Janet stood silent. *I'm not going*, she told herself, trying to make it sink in. Until one minute ago, she had been excitedly awaiting her sister's summons. Now her plans had instantly changed.

"I'm sorry, Janet," Mom sympathized. "I know you were really looking forward to going. I'm sorry it isn't working out the way you planned." Sweet Mom. Janet was grateful that she didn't add that it was going to be nice for seventeen-year-old Anna Williams to go, or that Sarah was being a submissive wife, or that God could use this to teach her a lesson. Janet knew all that, and at the moment she was just trying to adjust her thinking. *I guess I'll be teaching after all,* she realized.

"Well, that's that," she finally said, with an attempt at lightness. "I guess I don't need to pack."

Her voice caught, and she turned away, ashamed that she felt it so deeply.

Mom's arms went around her. "I love you, Janet," was all she said, but it helped.

So Janet kept teaching. She enjoyed the short visit to see little Esther, but somehow she didn't want to stay long, afraid Sarah would mistake her disappointment for bitterness. In truth, it was hard to leave the Williams children. Lydia cried when Janet put on her coat. "Danny, stay!" she wailed, and Janet wanted to cry, too. "I'll be back," she whispered, bending down to give her a hug. She wished she knew when that would be.

November 26

Just when I think I have God's will figured out, something comes up to change it. Take the issue of helping Sarah. I was sure that was how God wanted to use me – my "ministry," so to speak. Then He intervened, and showed me that I needed to be faithful to what He has given me here, serving Mom by teaching. I had a hard time surrendering to a change of plans, as earlier pages can attest, but got through that rough place, and was enjoying the work He had for me. I was really pretty contented.

Well, this afternoon Sarah called and talked to me for a while. She said Anna is leaving on Friday because they need her at home, but she could use help for another week or so, and would I be willing to come? I think she feels bad that she couldn't ask me at first. Mom and Dad discussed it this evening, and I'm leaving in the morning.

I should be really excited, and I am. At the same time I'm a little frustrated, because having given up this trip, I have completely thrown myself into teaching and I'm (finally!) having a lot of fun. In history class we just started reading a new book (we're taking a break from the textbook) and the girls and I are having the best time! Mom will have it finished by the time I get back. I wish I could be in two places at once! But it looks like God wants me at Luke and Sarah's for now, and I'll accept that. It seems ridiculous to have to "accept" what I wished for so much a couple of weeks ago! Why am I so contrary?

Walking in the door at Sarah Williams' house cured Janet's contrariness. Three ecstatic children ran to greet her, with shouts of "Aunt Janet!" and "Danny!" She hugged the boys and scooped up Lydia. "I'm so glad to be here!" she exclaimed. Then she caught sight of Anna, standing quietly in the kitchen doorway. The children seemed to have completely forgotten her existence, and Janet could imagine her hurt at being ignored after caring for them for two weeks. "Hi, Anna," she greeted, giving the younger girl a hug. "It's good to see you again."

Anna smiled, returning the hug. "I'm glad you could come," she said sincerely. "Sarah still needs help, and I know you'd like to spend some time here, too."

Janet was impressed with Anna's sweet spirit. She seemed to be genuinely glad for her, and the thought crossed Janet's mind that if the situation were reversed, she would probably not be as happy as

Anna. *I have such a long way to go,* she thought, humbled by Anna's example.

At supper, Luke told Janet that his brother Daniel would be coming the next day to take Anna back home. "He's planning to help me work on the furnace on Friday, and leave Saturday morning," he said. "So you girls will have some time to visit."

"Oh, good," she replied, giving Anna's hand a little squeeze. For some reason, she really wanted to get to know this sweet girl. Regretfully she admitted that she had always treated her with indifference, thinking of her as a little girl. Today she had realized that Anna was growing up. As the oldest girl in the family, she had matured early, and Janet suddenly found they had a lot in common.

Anna and Janet, sharing a room, talked late into the night. "We'd better go to sleep," Anna finally said, and Janet agreed.

"We don't want Sarah to have to do everything tomorrow because we are too tired," she laughed. Her last thought that night was, *I'm making a new friend.* It was a friend she would not have thought of on her own.

The girls did the housework together Friday morning. By eleven thirty, all the cleaning was finished and the children were playing quietly. Anna started lunch in the kitchen, while Janet did some laundry, smiling as she folded Lydia's little dresses and Esther's tiny sleepers. *We haven't had little clothes to fold for a while,* she thought. For a fleeting moment she recalled the wistfulness in Mom's eyes as she cradled Sarah's baby. Her thoughts were interrupted by a knock on the door. She started to answer it, remembering just in time that she wasn't at home. *Oops,* she thought, ducking back into the laundry room. A moment later she was very glad she had not opened the door, for she heard a man's voice greeting Sarah and Anna. Suddenly shy, she stood still, listening but not wanting to go into the kitchen. *It must be Daniel,* she thought.

"Nice to see you," he was saying. "Is the baby asleep?"

"Yes, but you can see her," Sarah replied, leading the way to the living room where Esther slept in the cradle. Unaccountably relieved that they were going the other way, Janet returned to her folding.

A few minutes later she heard footsteps outside the door, and turned just in time to see Daniel Williams coming in. He stopped, surprised.

"Janet?" he queried, as if uncertain that it was really her. "I . . . how are you?" He seemed flustered and unsure of himself.

"Hello, Daniel," Janet found herself saying, suddenly feeling poised and confident. After all, Daniel wasn't a stranger. "I'm fine, and you?"

Some of his embarrassment faded. "I'm fine, too. I guess I knew you would be here, but for some reason I didn't expect to run into you like this! Luke wanted me to bring his toolbox to the basement, and he said it was in here."

"It's right here," Janet pointed. "You aren't going to start before lunch, are you?"

"No, Anna told us it's almost time to eat, so we're just setting up."

After Daniel left, Janet stood thinking for a long moment. She hadn't seen Daniel for a few years, since he had been working when the two families got together, and the Williams had missed Jeff's wedding because of sickness. *He must be twenty-five now,* she reflected. *No, he's two years younger than Jeff, so I guess he's twenty-three.* He'd grown up a lot in the last three years. Well, that was to be expected. He had been the oldest at home for several years now, ever since his brother Andrew had married and moved to Montana. She found herself wondering what he was like. *Stop it,* she told herself firmly. *Just because he's the right age, don't get any ideas.* Funny she'd never considered him before.

Luke and Daniel ate quickly, then headed to the basement, where work on the furnace consumed most of their afternoon. After doing the dishes, Janet and Anna washed Sarah's kitchen floor, chattering like squirrels the whole time.

"Last winter our family went to Nebraska to visit Mom's parents," Anna said. "It was a lot of fun, but what a long drive!"

"That is a long way," Janet agreed. "My grandparents live in Oklahoma, and we went down to see them when I was twelve or thirteen. We haven't been able to leave the farm for that long in a while. But I remember thinking that we would drive forever! How do you pass the time in the car?"

"Well, we girls like to do handwork, like crocheting or knitting." Anna swished her rag in the bucket. "I tried tatting last time, but I didn't get too far."

"Tatting?" Janet questioned. "I'm just learning that myself. Did you bring yours along?"

"Yes, but I haven't had time to work on it much here. When we're done with the floor we can look at it, if you want. Do you have yours with you?"

"Actually, I do, but I'm sure you're far ahead of me!" Janet laughed. "Right now mine looks like . . . well, not much of anything!"

The conversation drifted from topic to topic, finally settling on the girls' dreams for the future. Anna shared her struggles of trusting God to bring her a mate in His timing.

"And even though I'm young, it's hard to wait," she added. "It doesn't help to have married siblings that are so happy in their new homes. I'm glad for them, but it just reminds me that I don't have anyone yet."

"Oh, that's me exactly!" Janet exclaimed. "And I start to wonder how I'm going to meet anyone. I mean, there's just no one, and when I think . . ." She stopped, confused. Red crept up her neck and into her cheeks, and she turned to rinse out her rag to hide her blushing. *How about Daniel?* The thought was unbidden, but insistent.

Anna didn't seem to notice. She continued the conversation, and Janet rejoined it with an effort. She changed the topic as quickly as possible, though. Somehow she didn't feel like discussing courtship right now. Her thoughts chased each other around and around. *I can't say there's no one now. Yes, I can. I don't know what he's like or if he's even interested in marriage. But he's a "possible possibility."* That was what Stephanie always asked – "Are there any possible possibilities?" *I wonder what he's like? I really don't know him at all.*

Luke and Daniel finished the plumbing a little before suppertime. Luke went upstairs to talk with Sarah, and Daniel entertained the children while Anna and Janet finished making supper. The girls laughed at the sounds coming from the direction of the living room. "Rrrrrm, rrrrrrm! Screeech!" Then Daniel's voice, "Oh, Noah, you ran over my house!" Giggles from Noah and Judah, then the car noises started again.

"Danny, Danny!" Janet's ears caught the sound at once, despite the racket. Drying her hands on a towel, she hurried to answer the summons. To her surprise, Lydia continued to repeat, "Danny! Look, Danny," despite seeing Janet in the doorway. She stood beside Daniel, who was engrossed in the game with the boys. Her constant refrain finally attracted his attention, and he admired the doll she wanted to show him.

"Does she call you Danny, too?" Janet asked. "That's her nickname for me, although I'm not sure where she came up with it."

Daniel laughed easily. "I guess we share a nickname, then," he replied. "That's pretty neat."

Janet thought it was, too, but she didn't want to say so. Instead, she told him, "We're about ready to eat. The boys should probably pick up the toy cars and wash their hands."

"Okay, boys, pitch in!" She smiled at the way he interacted with them. He really enjoyed children.

That evening after the children were in bed, the adults sat in the living room and caught up on each other's lives. Janet sat quietly listening most of the time, taking advantage of the opportunity to see more of Anna's personality, as well as observing Daniel. He had a good sense of humor and reminded her of Steve, and she found herself wanting to know him better. He seemed to be quite willing to talk to her, as well, and asked many questions about their family and life on the farm, trying to draw her into the conversation. She appreciated his efforts to include her, for it would be easy to feel like an outsider in this setting. *He seems like a caring person,* she thought. *I wonder what he would be like in a home of his own? I've always dreamed of opening up my home to hurting people. I wonder if he would do that?* What was she doing – evaluating him as a possible match again? *Stop it, Janet,* she told herself. *It's not time for that.* He was certainly a nice young man, though.

Chapter Seven

"Goodbye! It was so nice to spend time with you," Janet said, hugging Anna.

"Yes, I'm so glad we had an extra day," she returned. Then, shyly, she added, "I know I'm younger than you, but . . . would you like to write? If you're too busy, that's fine."

"I'd love to," Janet replied honestly. "You really don't seem much younger than me, and God has already used you to bless me."

Anna's eyes shone. "You've blessed me, too. I'll write first." With a quick squeeze, she was gone, waving at Sarah's children as she hurried down the sidewalk. Daniel said his goodbyes as well, but it seemed to Janet that he was reluctant to go. Or was it merely her imagination?

The time at Sarah's house passed quickly. While Janet fully enjoyed caring for the children, she found herself once again filled with thoughts of courtship and a home of her own. No doubt this was due in part to the fact that she was seeing Sarah live out her dreams. Sarah was so happy, so fulfilled as a wife and mother, so in love with Luke.

But Janet knew that part of her struggles came from thoughts of Daniel. She tried not to think of him, but for some reason Sarah kept mentioning him. She knew him fairly well, since he was her husband's brother, and she had many good things to say about him. She didn't say much about his faults, however.

At first Janet attributed this to charity, but later she wondered if perhaps Sarah was trying to portray him in the best light possible. *I remember doing that when James Locke was interested in courting Sarah*, she thought rather sheepishly. At the time she had truly wanted Sarah's happiness, and now she knew Sarah was aware of her desire to marry. *Maybe she sees Daniel as a possibility, too,* Janet thought, then gave herself a firm reminder not to get her hopes up. *I don't want to think about him until – and unless – I know he's serious about me.* As yet, she did not know if he had given her two minutes' thought.

It was a few days before Janet was to return home that Luke suggested she and Sarah take a walk together. "I know you haven't had much of a chance to talk without the children around," he observed. "And it's a nice warm day. Esther just went to sleep, so this is a good time."

Sarah and Janet agreed. Indeed, it was an unusually warm day for late November, and the sun shone brightly. Except for the dry brown leaves littering the sidewalk and crunching underfoot, it felt more like spring than almost winter. A car drove past, lifting the leaves and sending them swirling across the street like huge snowflakes. Janet still found it hard to believe that Sarah lived in town, and said so.

"I'm still a country girl at heart," her sister confided. "And sometimes I miss the farm so much I have to go somewhere alone and cry."

Janet turned wondering eyes on her. "Really? You seem so happy. I must confess I've been jealous of you for a while. You're married, and you have your own children . . ." A lump in her throat stopped her.

Sarah took her hand. "It's hard to wait, isn't it? Oh, I remember so well!"

Tears filled Janet's eyes. "How long will I have to wait? Sarah, I want to get married so much!" She paused, searching for the right words. "I just don't understand why God hasn't sent anyone. He has promised not to withhold any good thing from them that walk uprightly. I know I'm a sinner, but I'm trying to walk uprightly. Am I not good enough yet?"

"Oh, Janet." Sarah's own eyes were misty as she gazed at her younger sister. "Let's sit down on that park bench. I want to tell you something – quite a few things, actually."

The two young women walked slowly through the papery leaves and sat facing each other on the bench Sarah had pointed out.

"Janet," she began seriously, "first of all, it's not a question of being good enough, because the Bible says 'all our righteousness is as filthy rags.' We don't earn God's gifts – that's why they are called gifts! I don't deserve to be married any more than you."

"Then why is God withholding His gifts from me?" Janet asked. Her finger traced a pattern on the bench.

"He isn't, dear," Sarah replied gently. "You might not recognize all of them, but He is giving you blessings every day. Singleness itself is a gift from Him, a time when you can be very close to Him without all the distractions of marriage and motherhood."

"That's what all married people say," Janet replied tonelessly.

"They say it because it is true. I didn't understand it either, but now I see things from the married viewpoint, and I have a different perspective. I think God gives us singleness as a special time to prepare us for whatever lies ahead in life, by teaching us to lean on Him and not trust our own strength."

Janet was really listening now, her attention caught by the last sentence. That was the very lesson God had been impressing on her recently in regards to teaching. Somehow she had never applied the principle to the area of courtship.

"But what if I still have years to wait? Or what if God never sends someone?" she asked.

"That's what I am getting to," Sarah answered. "This is the most important thing to understand. A husband will not satisfy all your longings and make you completely happy, Janet. He can't, and he's not even supposed to. God has created us with a need for Him that can't be filled by anyone or anything else. And if you expect a husband or any other person to fulfil that need, not only will you be disappointed, but you will end up hurting that person, because you want something they cannot give you. I've had to learn that lesson the hard way, and I've hurt myself and Luke in the process."

"So what is the answer?" Janet probed.

"You have to learn to let the Lord be the absolute center of your life – your reason for living – whether single or married. I think one of the biggest temptations for a single person is thinking that a human relationship can solve all our problems. But the root of all our unhappiness is sin, and a person can't take that away. Only God can cleanse our hearts and supply our deepest need – the need for fellowship with Him."

"I think I understand," Janet said slowly. Her eyes were thoughtful. "I've never heard it explained just like that before."

Sarah wasn't through. "I want to give you a scripture to think about," she continued. "It's Psalm 37:4: 'Delight thyself also in the Lord; and He shall give thee the desires of thine heart.' If you think God is not fulfilling that promise, there must be a reason. First, perhaps you aren't delighting yourself in Him. Let Him be your portion and your joy, not outside circumstances. Secondly, maybe your desires aren't His best for you, and He wants to change them. Either way, the key is to be surrendered to His will and walking with Him daily."

Janet sat quietly, considering Sarah's words. *Is God my 'everything?'* she wondered. *I always say He is first in my life, but what do I really mean by that? Am I just trying to sound spiritual?*

"There's something I need to confess to you," Sarah admitted. " I guess I still haven't fully learned to trust God's timing either. When I saw you and Daniel together, I thought it would be nice if you would start courting. But it's not my place to help God direct your life, and I apologize for encouraging you to think about Daniel. I've probably made it harder for you! I do think he's a fine young man, but if God wants to bring you together He can do it without my help."

"Thanks, Sarah. I forgive you," Janet replied, managing to blush to the roots of her hair. "It's been hard for me not to think about him, but I just want God's will."

Sarah gave her hand a squeeze. "I know you do. Let's pray together before we go home, okay?" At Janet's nod, she closed her eyes and bowed her head. "Dear Lord, we thank You for Your love and grace. We thank You that You know what is best for us, and that You always accomplish Your will in Your way and Your timing. Help Janet to trust You completely with her future. Help her to seek You with her whole heart. Be her joy and strength. Be her portion, Lord. Show her that You are all-sufficient, and that all her needs are met in Christ. Thank You for always hearing us, and thank You for Janet's life, and her love for You. Please bless her. In Jesus' name, Amen."

Tears once again filled Janet's eyes. The prayer had contained nothing unusual, but she knew Sarah meant every word. A deep love for her sister welled up in her heart. "Oh, Sarah," she began. "Do you think . . . I know you're really busy, but could you find time to write?" She realized she was echoing Anna's request of a few days before.

"Of course I could," Sarah smiled. "What is a big sister for? But I'm a mother now, too," she added, glancing at her watch, "and there will be some hungry children waiting at home. I guess we'd better head back."

So it was that Janet returned to the McLean farm with more than memories of a special time. She carried the beginning of a new friendship, and the renewal of an old one. She also carried some new ideas to ponder.

Chapter Eight

"Oh, good!" Janet exclaimed, opening the mailbox and seeing the pile inside. "What a lot of mail!" She hoped there was something for her. A cold November wind whipped her skirts around her legs, and she hurried toward the house, flipping through the mail as she went. *Mostly catalogs . . . there's a bill . . .* Her face lighted up as she saw Stephanie's familiar handwriting stretched across the front of an envelope. *I do have something!*

She tore the letter open as soon as she reached the quiet of the girls' room.

Dear Janet,

Greetings in Jesus' name! I tried to call you last week, but your mom told me about your visit to Sarah's house, so I decided to write. I'm so glad you could go – I know how much you were looking forward to that! How are all your nieces and nephews?

Life here is about the same. We are getting ready for a big Thanksgiving day because Micah's whole family is coming for dinner. It will be so much fun! But I'm already dreading the dishes. ☺

Speaking of Micah, our courtship is going well at the moment. I never dreamed there could be so many ups and downs. I'm learning so much about relating to men! Micah looks at life from a whole different perspective, which can make for a lot of misunderstandings. Thankfully, we are developing much better communication skills, but we still have problems. Usually it's because he has said something that bothered me, but instead of telling him, I just hold it in. Then he doesn't understand why I seem distant. We are learning to talk through our problems, instead of letting them build! Please keep me in your prayers, as I know you do.

Janet, I just want to thank you for being such a supportive friend. I know I can always count on you to listen and pray for me, and I really appreciate you!

I have to close this letter now and get some work done. Write soon, and tell me what's happening in your life!

Your sister in Christ,

Stephanie

Janet folded the letter with a sigh. Somehow, it had not been as enjoyable as she had expected. "Tell me what's happening in your life," she repeated, her voice edged with disgust. "Well, Stephanie dear, nothing – just exactly nothing!" She was busy, of course, with the daily work involved in life on a farm, and she was still helping to teach her siblings. *But as far as her kind of "news" is concerned – there's nothing.* She turned to go downstairs, feeling discouraged and more than a little sorry for herself.

Something outside caught her attention. She looked closer, then, smiling in spite of herself, she hurried down the steps and into the living room.

"It's snowing!" she announced joyfully. Four people instantly looked out the window to verify her statement, each responding in characteristic fashion.

"Well, look at that," Ben commented. His eyes returned to the page he was reading before the end of his sentence.

"It's snowing! It's snowing! Hey Mom, guess what?" Samuel called enthusiastically, running from room to room. "Look outside, it's snowing!"

Steve stood up and stretched. "I'd better warm up my skiing muscles," he said. "Becky, do you think I could strap cardboard to my feet so I can practice?"

Becky giggled. "If you can find some! I'm going to find Rachel and tell her about the snow."

As Janet turned to leave the living room, she barely avoided a head-on collision with Samuel, who had completed his rounds.

"Janet, it's snowing," he told her breathlessly, forgetting that he originally heard the news from her.

Janet just laughed. "Yes, it is," she replied. No matter how old one was, the first snow was still exciting.

That evening the snow was still swirling down, filling in the uneven spots in the yard and piling up on the porch railing. Janet sat quietly by the window, enjoying the serenity of the night. Snowflakes sparkled in the glow of the porch light, falling down, down, down, tossed by the slightest breath of air. She knew each flake was unique and beautiful, and yet all ended up on the frozen ground, each indistinguishable from its neighbor. Life was sort of like that, she reflected. God made every person so different, but unless one took the time to really see people as individuals, the world was a mere mass of humanity. *But God doesn't forget that He made each person as a special creation. And all of us have our place in His plan for the world.* She wondered exactly what that place was for her. And, as so often in the past weeks, she wondered if her place was at a man's side. Tonight Janet didn't feel anxious about the future. She just watched the drifting snow, resting in the knowledge that God would work all things for her good.

But moods are fickle, prone to change with circumstances, and Janet's contentment vanished abruptly four days later. A phone call was all it took.

"Janet?" Stephanie's voice bubbled happily through the earpiece. "You'll never guess what happened!"

I probably can, she thought, but she asked anyway. "What happened?"

"I'm engaged! Oh Janet, I'm so excited!"

"Congratulations!" Janet heard herself saying, but all she could think was, *Lord, why her and not me?* She prayed that she would sound enthusiastic as Stephanie went on and on, for her heart was beginning to ache. She swallowed hard and tried to listen to what her friend was saying.

". . . so we're thinking early June. Of course, if he gets transferred later, the date may have to be changed, but he's thinking that he would have enough time this way to get everything set up." The conversation wasn't making much sense to Janet. "Did you know that his brother lives about twelve miles from there?"

"That's nice," Janet replied, hoping Stephanie would change the subject soon so she would understand what they were discussing.

"Well, anyway, I'll call you – or write you – as soon as I know more," Stephanie concluded. "I can hardly wait to start making wedding plans!"

"Yes, that will be fun," Janet agreed.

The phone call ended, and Janet sought the quiet solitude of her room. She sank down on a chair beside the window and closed her eyes, fighting back the tears.

"Dear Lord," she whispered, "I'm not trusting. Help me, Father! This is so hard!" Opening her eyes, she gazed at the cold, bare branches against the gray sky. *I knew she would be engaged soon,* she reasoned. *And I should just be glad for her.* Memories of all the times they had shared dreams of marriage washed over her, only to be followed by the realization that those conversations were things of the past.

The tears came then, as Janet thought of how her friendship with Stephanie had changed over the past months. They had been so close until Micah entered the picture. Then Stephanie's interest in Janet's life waned, her mind full of her own joys and sorrows. That was natural, Janet told herself. She wondered if Stephanie's marriage would further widen the gap between them. *But how can I complain when she is so happy? Her dreams are coming true.* The thought brought little comfort.

Drying her eyes, Janet again sought the Lord. "Help me to be truly happy for Stephanie," she prayed. "And help me to be stayed on You, not myself or my desires. Help me to trust You as I wait to see Your plan for my life." She didn't feel much better, but she knew God heard her prayer regardless of her emotions. She had honored Him with her actions.

Trusting God's timing did not get easier at once, however, for the next day Jeff and Jenny came for supper. Janet watched them, inwardly weeping as she saw the sparkle in their eyes when they looked at each other. *They're so happy,* she thought, her own hunger for marriage growing even stronger.

After supper Dad kindled a fire in the fireplace, and the McLeans gathered in the living room. The newlyweds sat side by side on the couch. Jenny whispered in Jeff's ear, and he smiled at her tenderly, his big hand enveloping hers.

"Jenny and I have something to announce," he said, his smile widening into a grin that crinkled the corners of his eyes. "There will be a new McLean sometime in early June."

The whole room erupted in cheers and congratulations, and Janet hoped her slightly shaky response was lost in everyone else's excitement. The lump in her throat was back again.

Winter settled firmly over Michigan. The days were very short now, and Janet's birthday fell on the shortest day of all – December 21. Birthdays were always festive occasions at the McLean house, and Janet's twenty-third was no exception.

"Happy birthday, Janet!" Becky greeted as soon as she opened her eyes.

"Thank you," she mumbled, smiling sleepily.

The table was bright with balloons and streamers, and Mom surprised Janet by making her favorite breakfast, apple pancakes. The delicious smell greeted her as soon as she came in from milking.

"Ummm," she said, sniffing appreciatively. Mom gave her a hug, spoon in hand.

"Happy birthday, sweetheart," she replied.

School went well, and the morning passed pleasantly. Samuel was excited about the birthday meal, the cake in particular. "I hope Mom puts a lot of frosting on it!" he said at least three times. Janet laughed, rumpling his hair. Boys were so much fun.

That afternoon, however, saw Janet in a different frame of mind. The house was fairly rustling with secrets and last-minute gift wrapping, and she decided to take a walk despite the chilly temperatures. "That will keep me out of mischief," she smiled, putting on her coat. "Make sure you have plenty of presents!"

Her playful mood vanished as soon as the door closed behind her. She had been cheerful all day, pushing aside any gloomy thoughts that tried to come, but once alone she could stop pretending. This birthday was depressing. She was twenty-three, and as far from starting her life as ever. *Twenty-three! At eighteen I was wondering how much longer I'd have to wait, and it's been five years now.* "You're still so young, dear," Mom had told her only this morning, but Janet felt her youth slipping away. She longed to marry and start her own family – now, while she was young and strong, while she was in her prime. *Are these years being wasted?* she wondered. *I want to give myself to my husband now, not wait until I'm old! I'm already feeling like a frustrated old maid,* she thought wryly.

Returning to the house, she tried to shake off her depressed feelings, and succeeded in enjoying the special birthday meal. She exclaimed over the cards and gifts, and led the treasure hunt for the last present with the enthusiasm of a ten-year-old. No one seemed to guess the thoughts that were just under the surface, and for a while Janet almost forgot them herself.

When she went up to bed, however, her former mood returned. Rachel had lighted a jar candle, probably as one last birthday surprise, and the soft light illuminated the room. Somehow its serene glow seemed out of place tonight. Janet sat on the edge of her bed, thinking.

Lord, will I always be alone? she questioned silently, her heart heavy. *Will I become dried-up and withered, and never know the joy of sharing my life with a man? Will I grow old alone?* Yes, she had a loving family, but there was a deep hunger in her heart for something else. The candle shone steadily, but the quiet light only served as a contrast to her discontentedness. Almost fiercely she blew out the candle.

In mid-January there was a severe cold snap, and the mercury in the thermometer huddled pitifully at the bottom, not venturing above zero for several days. Ben got a touch of frostbite when he stayed out too long, and even Steve's normally high spirits drooped when a waterline broke.

"I wish those steers could just eat snow for a while," he grumbled, tugging on an extra pair of wool socks. "I guess I'll have to haul water for them."

Janet bundled up and went out with him. The frosty breath of the morning clung to every branch and twig, sending glints of sunlight into their eyes. Together they walked to the tractor, the hard, crusty snow squeaking underfoot.

"Sure hope this old thing starts today," Steve grinned. He felt better about the situation since Janet was there to face the cold with him. He turned the key and held it for a moment, warming up the combustion chamber on the old diesel Ford. "Well, here goes." He twisted the key once more, and the tractor sputtered to life, coughing up black puffs of smoke in the frigid air. Steve flashed a grin and a thumbs up to Janet.

She returned the signal. "Praise the Lord!" she shouted, although her voice was covered by the sound of the engine. Steve drove slowly through the snow, the tires slipping in icy spots, and Janet helped him hitch up the "water wagon," a large tank welded to an old trailer. It worked well in the summer when they hauled water to the far pastures, but winter was another story. Water splashed from the opening in the top as they jolted over the uneven ground, forcing Janet to seek a drier seat. Once at the water trough, the thirsty steers jostled the trailer impatiently, sending water cascading to the ground, where it immediately froze in sheets of glass. Steve, his normal good humor restored, suggested that Janet try ice-skating to get warm.

"Take lessons from that big guy," he laughed, pointing at a large steer who was trying – rather unsuccessfully – to navigate the slippery surface.

On the way back to the barn, Janet sat on the back of the trailer, her feet dangling over the whiteness of the field. The noise of the tractor was muted somewhat, and she watched the trees receding in the distance. *Sure is cold,* she thought, shivering as the wind found a way into the collar of her coat. It was quite a contrast from the hay-making heat of July. If only that scorching heat would sweep across her face for a few minutes! Then she had to laugh at herself. *In the summer I'd give anything for a chilly breeze like this. Why can't I ever be content with what I have? When will I learn to take each day from God's hand, just the way He ordains it?* As usual, her thoughts turned to marriage. *I know that applies to waiting for the right man, too.* She sighed, hoping it wouldn't be too long. Lately she had begun to feel she would be single forever.

Chapter Nine

As the winter wore on, Janet's struggle for contentment grew more intense, or perhaps the temptations were just getting stronger. Sometimes she wondered if she was really trying to be content. Perhaps her turmoil came from just wanting her own way. She wanted to be married so much, and nothing was happening. *I think I'll call Anna this afternoon,* she thought. *I'm not sure I can handle talking to Stephanie today, and hearing about how wonderful Micah is.* She waited until supper preparation was underway, then dialed the Williams' number.

"Hello," a man's voice greeted.

"Hello, is Anna there? This is Janet McLean," she replied.

"Oh, hello, Janet! This is Daniel. How are you?"

"I'm fine," she said, half-hoping that he would keep talking. She had enjoyed their conversation at Luke and Sarah's house, and besides, it was unusual – and exciting – for her to be talking to a young man on the phone without a real reason.

Daniel didn't seem to be in a hurry to get Anna. "So, what have you been up to?" he asked. "It's been pretty cold up there, hasn't it?"

"Yes, it's been really cold!" she answered, proceeding to tell him about the broken water pipe. He seemed to enjoy the story, and laughed about the steer on the ice.

"We've had some ice, too," he told her. "But not enough for Hope and Beth. They want to ice skate every day, so Jonathan and I made a small skating rink for them."

"Oh, how nice!" Janet exclaimed. "I'm sure they love that. How did you make it?"

"Well, first we tried just mounding up snow around the edge of a depression in the yard, but that didn't work," Daniel answered. "Then we used a sheet of plastic on the bottom, and that helped a lot."

They continued to talk for a while, and Janet enjoyed every minute of the conversation. Daniel was so friendly, and so genuinely interested in everything she had to say. When he finally remembered that she had called to talk to Anna, twenty minutes had passed.

Well, that was a unique experience! Janet thought, still excited, as she returned to supper preparation. *I never knew I would enjoy talking to someone like that! Daniel is so nice.* Again she remembered that evening at Sarah's house, and she wondered if she would get another chance to talk to him. He was someone she could easily imagine becoming friends with . . . *and he's the right age,* she thought. Well, one never knew how things might work out. The thought crossed her mind that perhaps she should tell her parents of this conversation, but she dismissed it. *What is there to tell?* she reasoned. *I didn't call to talk to him, and we really didn't talk about anything. It's not like there's any news they would like to hear.* And she really didn't want to share the memory of that phone call with anyone, anyway. It was special, and she wanted to just treasure it alone.

But that phone call had unforseen consequences for Janet. She had already been thinking about Daniel as a 'possible possibility,' although she tried not to. Now that she had again talked to him, and found that he was just as nice as she had remembered, it was harder. Over the next weeks, thoughts of Daniel plagued her, and she found her attraction to him growing, even though she had no more direct contact with him. Anna's newsy letters were full of all her family, but it seemed to Janet there was always something interesting about Daniel, and she found herself re-reading those parts and pouring over the pictures Anna innocently sent.

"What am I doing?" she asked herself in frustration one day. "Why am I allowing myself to even think about him? I never wanted to form any kind of attachment with a young man except my future husband, and I have no indication that I will ever marry Daniel. Have I ruined everything I fought for so long? Have I failed to guard my heart?" She felt confused, and unsure of what she should do with her feelings. Until that time, she had kept her thoughts strictly to herself, but recently she had felt increasingly uneasy about the situation.

I ought to tell Mom and Dad, she admitted. *But that won't be easy. How do you go about something like that? Just say, 'Hey Dad, I'm really attracted to Daniel Williams'? That would be so awkward!* How she hated the thought of trying to explain! They would be disappointed at what a failure she was. *You're a girl who is supposedly committed to courtship*, she thought grimly. *Well, you've ruined everything now.* She knew that waiting would not make things easier, however, and she determined to talk to her parents that evening.

Her opportunity came after the chores were done for the evening. Mom was sewing, and Dad sat beside her idly paging through a farm catalog. They looked up and smiled as Janet entered the room.

"Can I talk to you?" she began hesitantly.

"Of course, Janet," Dad answered, laying aside the catalog. "We always have time to talk to you."

Janet took a seat rather self-consciously. "I need to tell you something, and I don't know how to start!" She laughed nervously, wishing it could already be over.

"Don't worry," Mom comforted. "Just go ahead and tell us."

"We can always ask questions to clarify," Dad added. "Don't be afraid to share whatever it is."

Janet took a deep breath. "Well, it's not anything horrible," she said. "Do you remember how I told you about Daniel Williams coming to pick up Anna when I was at Sarah's house?" *What a ridiculously long sentence!* she thought as she paused for breath and courage. "Well, I didn't tell you that . . . well, I . . . um, he's really nice, and I think I'm getting attracted to him." There! It was out. Her face felt red.

Mom and Dad exchanged relieved glances. "I'm so glad you told us, Janet," Dad said, breaking the silence. "I know that wasn't easy."

"Do you want to explain a little more about how this happened?" Mom questioned gently.

"I don't really know," Janet replied. "When I saw him at Sarah's house, I couldn't believe how much he had grown up. He's changed and matured a lot since I saw him last. He's . . . very nice." She felt herself blushing again, and Mom looked at her intently.

"You haven't been in contact with him since, have you?" she asked seriously.

"No . . . that is, not really," Janet answered. "I called the Williams to talk to Anna a few weeks ago, and he answered the phone, but we only talked for a little while." She hesitated, then continued, "I guess I should have told you that before, but I didn't. I'm sorry."

"We forgive you," Dad said. "You're right, though. It would have been wise to tell us right away. In fact, anytime there is something that you want to keep to yourself like that, you should see that as a warning."

"A warning?" Janet echoed. "What do you mean?"

"You probably didn't want to tell us about the phone call because it was special and exciting, right?" Mom questioned. At Janet's nod, she continued, "That's a warning that your heart might be going in a direction that isn't wise. Keeping things like that to yourself tends to make you continue to dwell on them, and they start to seem even more significant than they really are. If you tell Dad and I, that will help it seem less 'special' and you'll be able to have a more realistic view of things."

"Maybe that's one reason that my attraction has increased lately," Janet pondered aloud. "It's getting very hard not to think about him, even though I have no indication that he is interested in me." She shared how even Anna's letters were a source of struggle. "And I find myself trying to make my letters sound very spiritual. I've realized that I do it because I hope he will hear them, and be impressed with me, and I know that is wrong."

Thoroughly disgusted at the recital of her sins, Janet looked up to see her parents' reaction. To her surprise, both were smiling. "Janet, I can't tell you how much maturity you are showing. It takes a lot of courage to confess things like that, especially because we might never know if you didn't tell us."

Dad was responding in a very different way than she had expected. Wasn't he going to say she should have guarded her heart and then this wouldn't have happened? She was amazed at his next words. "It would have been even better to come to us sooner, but you are doing the right thing now. Telling Mom and I was an important part of guarding your heart, because now we can offer counsel and pray for you. We can also keep abreast of any developments." He smiled at her.

"But Dad!" Janet protested. "Am I guarding my heart? If I was, I shouldn't have even had the first thought about him, right?"

It was Mom's turn to smile. "God made us to desire marriage, and part of that is being attracted to people," she said. "It's not a sin for the thoughts to enter your mind. The next step is deciding what to do with those thoughts and emotions, and now you are choosing the right path."

"I thought I had ruined my chance for a perfect courtship story," Janet admitted, with a sigh of relief.

"Don't expect a perfect story in this fallen world," Mom warned. "But you are doing what you should. Now you have to continue to guard your heart, and not let your emotions get carried away. That won't be easy."

"We will help you all we can," Dad interjected, "but this is something we can't do for you. It will be your battle, and only you can fight it. The Lord will help you, and you can always come to us for advice. We'll be praying for you, too."

"Thanks, Dad," Janet returned gratefully. "I know it won't be easy, but I want to do what's right."

"That's the right attitude," Mom encouraged. "God will bless you for that, Janet."

"Let's pray about this right now," Dad suggested. Bowing his head, he began, "Heavenly Father, we thank You that You give wisdom to Your children. We ask that You would bless Janet as she trusts You for her future, and we pray especially that You would guard her heart. Help her to save her emotions for her future husband, and help her to leave Daniel in Your hands. We know that You have a perfect plan for each of them, and we pray that Janet would cling to that as she goes through this difficult time of life.

"And Lord, we pray for Janet's future husband, whoever that may be. We ask You to keep him for her, and that he would be pure, and following You with all his heart. Bring them together in Your time, we pray. In Jesus' name, Amen."

"Thank you," Janet said softly. She wanted to say more, but couldn't get the words out. She wasn't even sure what she wanted to say, so she hugged her parents and left the room. Mom and Dad watched her go.

"No, it won't be easy," Mom repeated.

Janet was glad she had confided in her parents, because she knew it was right. She felt much better about the situation, now that they were aware of it and could pray for her. Still, the difficulties only increased. It seemed to Janet that simply talking about her problem had opened the way for a veritable flood of thoughts that must be battled. Three days later, she reached for her journal out of desperation.

February 4

I know I did the right thing in telling Mom and Dad about Daniel, but it seems like that only made it harder! Now it's a conscious effort ***not*** *to think of him. I can't seem to find anything else to focus on, and it frustrates me to no end.*

My biggest temptation right now is to tell people, although I know it's not time yet. I want to tell Stephanie so badly! Why? Maybe it's because I want to feel like I have a possibility (although I know nothing of the kind). Or maybe it's just that I want sympathy. At any rate, it's hard to write letters that are supposed to tell her "what's going on" in my life without mentioning Daniel. But if I'm honest with myself, I'll admit there's still nothing going on in my life, just in my heart and mind! Oh dear. This is not a fun position. When I was about sixteen, I couldn't wait to grow up and deal with these issues – but I never thought it would be like this.

She closed the book and sat thinking. She had far more questions than answers. How was she supposed to go about guarding her heart? How could she banish Daniel from her thoughts? Why would God allow her to be attracted to him when there was no evidence that the feeling was returned? *God must have something for me to learn,* she reflected. *He has a purpose in everything, and He can use this in my life.*

Chapter Ten

"Oh, no!" Becky's giggle greeted Janet as she entered the sewing room. "Did I sew the pocket to the bottom of the skirt?" She held up a confusing tangle of loose threads and odd-shaped pieces of fabric. "Janet, where *is* the top of this?"

Janet laughed, too. "However did you manage that, child?" she teased. "Let me take a look at it." She lifted the skirt to the window where the light was better. "This is the top," she said, pointing. "Your pockets are here . . . this is where the waistband goes . . . You're doing fine!" She smiled at her youngest sister. The girls had recently shown an interest in learning to sew, and Mom and Janet were helping each of them make a simple skirt.

"Good." Becky sighed with relief. "I thought I had ruined it."

"Oh, there's always the seam ripper," Janet reassured her, with a twinkle in her eye. "And how are you doing, Rachel?"

"Well . . ." Rachel replied slowly, concentrating on the half-finished skirt in her lap. "I'm using the seam ripper!" She looked up and managed a smile. "I can't seem to get this to fit, and I've tried it several times."

Janet sat down beside her. "Do you know why it won't fit, dear?" she asked gently. "You are trying to put the wrong pieces together. Here, let me show you."

"No wonder it didn't work!" Rachel exclaimed a moment later, when Janet had the pieces properly pinned. "Janet, if you hadn't helped me, it wouldn't have been a skirt at all. It would have been a tent!"

All the girls laughed. "A very small tent," Rachel amended, giggling. "Or maybe a big lampshade."

Mom entered the room amid a fresh burst of laughter. "Sounds like you're having fun," she said. "Are you making progress, too?" She smiled, enjoying the sight of her daughters working together.

"We're making good progress now," Becky assured her. "And now that Janet is here, we're making skirts again, instead of tents or lampshades." All the girls went off into gales of laughter again.

The four McLean ladies worked together for an hour and a half. Mom and Janet didn't get much done on their own projects, because the younger girls needed a lot of teaching and supervision, but they all had a wonderful time.

"Janet, do you know what time it is?" Mom questioned, looking at her watch. "I'm afraid you're going to have to go make supper."

Janet looked at her own watch. "Four o'clock already? I'll have to hurry. I think I can have supper ready by five thirty."

"We'll miss you," Becky called as Janet hurried from the room. She smiled, calling back, "I'll see you sometime soon!" *I'm so glad I can work with my sisters,* she thought. *They are so much fun.*

"Supper time!" Janet called a while later, pulling a pan of scalloped potatoes out of the oven. Mentally she ran down the list: roast, potatoes, carrots, rolls, applesauce. The table was set, the glasses filled with water. *I think I'll light some candles,* she decided. The sun set so early in the winter that it had been dark for an hour already, and the warm glow of candlelight would make the meal more cheery.

In a few minutes' time, everyone except Dad had appeared. They gathered around the table, casting hungry glances at the steaming dishes.

"Dad is on the phone, so I think we'll go ahead and have the blessing without him," Mom informed them. "He's been talking for quite awhile, and it sounds like they are having a good time. I think we will get a report when he comes down." She smiled at the curious faces.

"Do you know who it is?" Rachel questioned eagerly.

"I can't say." Mom's eyes twinkled. "Ben, will you ask the blessing, please?"

Dad did not join his family at the supper table for nearly twenty minutes, and when he arrived, everyone stopped talking and waited expectantly. He pretended not to notice at first, but when he looked up from buttering a roll and saw fourteen eyes watching him, he laughed and relented.

"So, do you want to know who I was talking to?" he asked nonchalantly. At the chorus of assenting voices, he continued, "That was the phone company."

"Oh, Dad," Janet remonstrated. "We know that can't be it!"

"It was," he insisted. "I had a question about a bill." Then, seeing the crestfallen faces surrounding the table, he added, "But just before that, I was talking to Mr. Williams. Mr. *Mark* Williams. They are coming for a visit."

The expectant quiet was shattered by a babble of excited voices. Except through Anna's and Janet's letters they hadn't been in contact with Luke's family for quite some time, and everyone had something to say. Everyone but Janet, that is. She sat quietly, trying to appear normal, but a thousand thoughts went through her mind in those moments. *Why would Mr. Williams call? Did it have anything to do with my letters? He hasn't talked to Dad on the phone for a long time. What made him suddenly decide to call? And why are they coming to visit out of the blue like this?* And, although she did not want it, the thought came: *Could it be that Daniel wants them to get to know me again?* She tried to enter the conversation.

"When are they coming?" she asked, hoping the question had not been raised already.

"Not until the middle of April," Dad replied. "Mr. Williams has several vacation days, but he can't get them all together until then."

The middle of April. That would be about a month and a half, Janet calculated. Her thoughts started again. *Why are they coming all of a sudden? Are they checking things out for a courtship?* She knew she shouldn't be thinking like this, but it seemed impossible to quiet her thoughts. *Dear Lord, help me to honor You with my thoughts,* she prayed. *Don't let me run ahead of Your plans or get my hopes up.*

The next six weeks seemed to drag on forever, but excitement ran high. The plans grew to include Jeff and Jenny, as well as Luke, Sarah, and their children.

"Sounds like a regular McLean-Williams reunion," Dad commented one morning in early April. He consulted a letter in his hand. "Mark says that Andrew and his wife . . . let's see, what was her name?... oh, yes, Debbie . . . anyway, they might be able to come, too."

"All the way from Montana?" Mom was surprised. "That's a long way!"

"Yes, it is," Dad agreed, "and they may not make it, but they are trying to work everything out. We sure will have a full house."

"Jenny offered to have some people at their place," Mom told him. "But I know she isn't feeling very well, so I'd rather have everyone here if we can all fit."

"I think we can," Dad said. "It will be tight, but that's okay. It's only for a few days."

Janet looked up with a little smile. Normally Dad disliked being crowded. "I need elbow room," he would say, to which Samuel always responded, "Just like Daniel Boone!" She was glad for his willingness to sacrifice his comfort for the good of others.

"If we really can't fit, maybe a few of the adults can go to Jenny's," she suggested. "That wouldn't make as much work for her."

"Good idea," Dad assented. He turned to leave the room, then stopped short, staring out the window. "What is going on out there?" he muttered.

Mom joined him. "Oh, Janet, you'd better call the boys!" she exclaimed. "It looks like a lot of the cows are out."

Chasing the cows back to their proper place took nearly half an hour, and Janet was winded when it was over. *This isn't the way I had planned to spend the morning,* she thought, as she held a piece of fencing in place so Steve could repair it. *At least it isn't too cold.* The sun, although still weak, shone hopefully on the snow banks, promising that spring was on the way. Mom knew it, too, and the upcoming visit had spurred her to start "spring cleaning" a month earlier than usual.

"I think Mom is like a bird or something," Steve had commented one day. "She thinks of things like that at the same time every year."

Mom just smiled. "Yes, dear," she responded. "It must be a mother's instinct!"

"It's a good thing she has that instinct," Ben said loyally. "If the cleaning was left up to the guys, it might never get done!"

Janet jumped as Steve gave the fence post one more blow with his hammer. "There, that should hold it," he declared. "Ready to go inside?"

"We probably should," she agreed. "Mom wanted me to wash the bedroom floors this morning."

Steve squinted at the sun. "Well, it's only about nine thirty, so you should have time for that. Just be sure someone stops working in time to make lunch!"

Besides the cleaning, Janet was still teaching. She was really enjoying it now, and had learned many ways to make her job go more smoothly. Often she could start the girls on their math, then let them work on their own while she did other things. She tried to be available to answer questions, although recently they had fewer things they did not understand. Becky, especially, had begun to figure out new concepts on her own.

Rachel's strong subject remained history, and Janet was amazed at her memory. She would hear her sister telling Samuel story after story, filling in the outlines from the history book with details gleaned from biographies and other books she'd read. When Rachel told a story, everyone in the area tried to listen in.

By the second Sunday in April, the house was clean from top to bottom, and the barn had been cleaned and straightened, too. Less than a week remained until the "Grand Reunion," as Steve had dubbed it, and rumors were frequent and numerous as plans changed. Andrew and Debbie would not be able to come, but there was much discussion as to possible activities. Samuel thought they should all go canoeing.

"In *April*?" Janet laughed. "Samuel, we'd get frostbite!" She was finding it easy to laugh these days, her spirits soaring at the prospect of spending time with Luke and Sarah, her beloved nieces and nephews, Anna . . . and Daniel, although she didn't want to admit the last one even to herself. She caught herself thinking of him too often, and twice she had realized that she was planning a deep conversation with him. *As if I'd actually do that!* she thought, flabbergasted at the treachery of her mind. But she felt warm and happy when she remembered his smile. *I'll see it again soon,* she thought – then gave herself a good scolding. She was disgusted at herself, and her frustration was intensified this morning because they would be leaving for church momentarily, and she wanted desperately to have her mind fixed on the Lord and spiritual things. *Lord, help me,* she pleaded, picking up her Bible and joining the others on the porch. *Don't let my mind wander this morning.*

The service was a blessing, as always. Janet was grateful for the opportunity to fellowship with other believers, and the sermons were full of Biblical admonitions. This Sunday the sermon seemed especially applicable. The text was found in Romans 12:1-2, but as the pastor explained, the passage really started several verses earlier, at the end of chapter eleven.

"We'll start in verse thirty-three," he said, turning the pages of his Bible. After reading the entire passage, he began to expound verse by verse. This was Janet's favorite kind of sermon, and she took notes as he spoke.

"'Oh the depth of the riches both of the wisdom and knowledge of God! how unsearchable are his judgements, and his ways past finding out!' We don't have to understand the 'why' behind everything He does. In fact, with our human limitations, we really can't understand the reasons for everything. But His judgments are unsearchable – they are perfect, without mistakes.

"'For who hath known the mind of the Lord? or who hath been his counsellor?' He has all wisdom. We can never come close to attaining the wisdom He has, and we certainly can't add to His wisdom. 'Or who hath first given to him, and it shall be recompensed unto him again?' God gave us everything – our salvation, possessions, time, and our very existence! He doesn't owe us anything, and we can't give Him anything that didn't originate with Him.

"'For of him, and through him, and to him are all things: to him be glory both now and forever . Amen.' That's a pretty straightforward summary of the past few verses. The passage continues in chapter twelve, with 'I beseech you therefore, brethren, that ye present your bodies a living sacrifice . . .' We feel that at least our bodies are our own! But Who do they really belong to? We are to offer them up as a living sacrifice. I want you to notice two things here. First, it is a sacrifice. That means it's not easy. But that shows God that we really do want to please Him, and that we are willing to do whatever He wants. Secondly, it is a 'living' sacrifice. That means we must offer God our bodies day by day for His service."

Janet was scribbling notes as fast as possible. Her pen seemed to be running out of ink, so she got another out of her purse. She wanted to get this all down.

"The verse tells us a few more things about this sacrifice," the pastor went on. "It says it is 'holy, acceptable unto God, which is your reasonable service.' We aren't heroes for doing this. It's only right. Again, God really 'owns' us already. 'And be not conformed to this world' – which says you have the right to 'be yourself' and do whatever you please. We are to be different, 'transformed by the renewing of your mind.' This is an internal change, not merely the external works. When our minds are renewed, we can show the world how God wants us to live. That's why the verse ends with, 'that ye may prove what is that good, and acceptable, and perfect, will of God.'

"Do you want to please God? Do you want to show the world what it means to be a Christian? Then I encourage you to ask the Lord to show you ways to present your bodies a living sacrifice. For some people, that means accepting physical problems. For others, it means working hard at whatever job He has given you, be it providing for your family, caring for your children, nursing an elderly parent, or ministering to your siblings."

Her page full of notes, Janet closed her Bible. What a lot to think about! *I can already see some ways this applies to me,* she contemplated. *I've been thinking too much about my wants, not about what God wants from me. Maybe the sacrifice He wants from me is just accepting my singleness.* The thought stayed with her all day.

Chapter Eleven

Janet gave herself one more searching look in the mirror. Her heart was pounding and her hands trembled. *You're being ridiculous,* she told herself, but it didn't help. The Williams had arrived an hour earlier than expected, and she was summoning her courage as the others congregated at the front door. She heard the excited babble begin as the guests came up the sidewalk and through the open front door. She couldn't stay upstairs any longer. With a wordless prayer, she hurried downstairs to join the others in the crowded entryway.

There seemed to be a hundred people in the small area, all talking and laughing at once, taking off shoes and coats, and trying to catch up on all the family news. Janet greeted Anna with a hug, then began collecting coats to take to the schoolroom. She felt a desperate need for action. She stooped to pick up a hat, and when she straightened back up, there was Daniel. Their eyes met for a brief moment, and he smiled, his face lighting up.

"Hello, Janet!"

"Hi, Daniel," she replied. "Can I take your coat?" Too late she realized how silly that sounded, since he was standing there holding his coat out to her. She took it and hurried away, her ears burning. He had spoken to her, had smiled at her! He seemed very glad to see her, and she didn't even try to quell the excitement she felt.

Both families gathered in the living room, the adults and older children talking, the younger ones a bit uncertain and shy. Mr. Williams had a little more gray in his beard, Janet noticed, surveying the guests with interest. Although they saw the Williams occasionally, it had been almost two years since the last time they were together, and the younger children, especially, had changed and matured. Mrs. Williams was as sweet as ever. She and Mom were already engaged in earnest conversation, nodding and smiling as they talked about the dearest people in the world to them – their families.

Daniel had his back to Janet, and she took advantage of the opportunity to observe him for a moment without his knowledge. He wasn't as tall as dark-haired Matthew, but his bearing was confident. His hearty laugh rang out often as he got reacquainted with Ben and Steve. Matthew must be twenty-two now. He had always seemed to be on the serious side, and Janet remembered that he was the most studious of the boys.

Jonathan had changed the most. The first time Janet could remember meeting the Williams was almost eight years earlier, the memorable start of a chain of events that led to Luke and Sarah's marriage. Jonathan had been small for his age, with a limp due to a birth defect. Quiet and shy, he had reminded Janet of a little mouse, ready to flee if threatened. Now, at age nineteen, he was like a different person. His limp was still noticeable, although Janet wondered if that was only because she was looking for it. The first thing people noticed about him now was his big smile. He was one of the happiest people Janet had ever seen, and seemed completely unaware of any physical problems. Later, Anna was to tell Janet of Jonathan's absolute acceptance of God's will for his life, and the love and compassion he had for those in pain, whether physical, mental, or emotional.

She turned her attention to the girls. Anna was so much like her mother that Janet had to smile. Right now she was telling Rachel about the trip, and her voice and mannerisms were nearly identical to those of Carol Williams. Hope was fifteen, and quite as talkative as Becky. Beth was still as quiet as ever. She and Becky, although opposite in personality, were very close in age – both would turn twelve in June.

"Girls, would you like to go outside?" Janet suggested, joining the conversation. "It's a beautiful day, and we have some new calves in the pasture."

Quiet Beth responded at once. "Yes, let's go see them!" She loved animals.

The boys had just decided to go out, too, so they all headed to the pasture together. The cows, enjoying the spring sunshine, were trying to graze, although the grass was still brown and there were remnants of snow banks in the hollows.

"Oh, how sweet!" Hope exclaimed, reaching through the fence to pet the soft head of the most inquisitive calf.

"That's Juniper," Ben informed her. "We're naming the calves after trees this year. That one is Birch," he added, pointing, "and those three are Poplar, Aspen, and Maple. We want to –"

He was interrupted by a honking horn. A blue minivan slowly drove up the driveway and stopped in front of the house. The greetings started all over again as Luke, Sarah, and their children got out of the car and stretched their stiff muscles.

"Hi, everyone!" Luke said, helping Noah out and unbuckling Lydia's car seat. Five-year-old Judah jumped out by himself, and immediately ran over to Samuel.

"Let's go do something!" he said by way of greeting. Everyone laughed.

"Go hug the grandmas before you disappear on us," Luke chuckled. Sarah had already carried a sleepy Esther into the house.

"Danny! Hi, Danny!" Lydia shrieked, running to Janet's open arms. She hugged the little girl, brushing back her wispy hair.

"Does this 'Danny' get a hug?" Daniel asked, pausing on his way to the house with a suitcase. He smiled at Janet. He hadn't forgotten that they shared a nickname. She returned the smile.

At supper, Janet got a glimpse of another side of Daniel's personality.

"So, Daniel," Luke was saying, "has Dad figured out what he's going to do about the porch floor yet?"

"Yes, he wants me to crawl under there and replace about half the joists," he replied.

Luke's eyes twinkled. "And knowing you, I'm sure you can't wait to start."

Daniel grinned back. "Well, that was last fall. I guess I'll have to start pretty soon, but it's still cold. I'll do it when it warms up."

"After all the mud is gone," Anna said, joining the conversation. To Janet, who was sitting next to her, she added in a low tone, "Daniel is a notorious procrastinator."

"Everyone is different," Janet answered, thinking of his hardworking brother, Luke.

"Yes," Anna agreed, under the cover of the children's chatter. "But the problem is that most jobs wait until Luke or Andrew come home for a visit, or Dad just does it himself. I wish Daniel would take more responsibility."

Oh, well, Janet thought. *He'd probably be different if it was his own house.*

After the dishes were washed and the evening chores done, Dad suggested that they all gather in the living room to sing. "Too bad Jeff and Jenny aren't with us tonight," he said, passing out songbooks as everyone tried to find a place to sit. "They planned to come for supper tonight, but Jenny wasn't feeling well, so they'll come tomorrow."

Soon the living room was filled with praise, as the Williams and McLean families joined in worship. Dad suggested a few songs, then others started choosing as well. Janet, sitting beside Sarah, paged through the songbook looking for "Redeemed." She thought it was around number 200, but she couldn't remember. Just as she found it, she heard Daniel say, "How about number 211 – 'Redeemed.'"

She glanced up in surprise, and their eyes met briefly again. Blushing, she looked away in confusion. She was glad when the singing began. *That's quite a coincidence,* she thought. *Of course, he didn't know that was the song I was thinking of, but it's pretty special just the same.*

The evening passed quickly, and soon it was time to get everyone settled for bed. The McLean house was full, but everyone found a place to sleep – some in sleeping bags, some on couches, and a few in beds. Luke, Sarah, and their children had the girls' room, so Janet and her younger sisters, as well as the three Williams girls, spread blankets on the kitchen floor.

"We'll have to get up early in the morning so no one steps on us," Rachel commented, smoothing her pallet beside Hope's.

"Well, the sun will come in that window and wake us up," Becky said, pointing. "And then we can all make breakfast."

"Someone will have to milk the goats, right?" Beth asked hopefully. Janet read the question in her eyes.

"That's right," she smiled. "Would you like to come out and help me tomorrow morning?"

"Oh, yes!" Beth replied eagerly. "That is, if I'm not needed in the house to help with breakfast."

"The four of us can probably handle it," Anna assured her. "But we'd better settle down for the night now."

Anna is so conscientious, Janet contemplated half an hour later. Talk had died out, and the even breathing around her showed that most people were asleep. But sleep evaded her. Scenes from the afternoon replayed themselves in her mind, and most centered around Daniel. She knew she shouldn't be thinking about him, but in the quietness her thoughts chased each other around and around. *He sure is a nice person,* she thought. *And I have two days to get to know him better! I wonder what he thinks of me?* At last she drifted into pleasant dreams.

Chapter Twelve

The next morning promised to turn into a warm day. On the way back from the barn, Janet spied a dandelion lifting its bright face to the sun. "Look, Beth!" she exclaimed. "The first flower of the season! We should take the little ones on a walk today."

"That would be nice," Beth agreed. "And I'm sure they would enjoy seeing the new goat kids, too."

The kitchen was like a beehive. Mom directed the food preparation, while Mrs. Williams and Becky set the table. Anna and Rachel were buttering stacks of toast, and Hope was cooking a huge skillet of scrambled eggs. When the guys came in, the kitchen got even more crowded. They milled around "like cattle waiting for hay," Dad said, and peeked under lids, sampled toast, and asked repeatedly, "How long until breakfast?"

"If you go sit down it will be done sooner," Mom assured them laughingly. "We have a little too much help!"

Soon after breakfast, Janet approached her older sister. "Sarah, can we girls borrow your children?" she asked.

"Borrow my children?" she echoed. "For how long?"

"We want to take them outside to look for signs of spring," Janet explained. "It's nice and warm, and I wanted to take them to that south-facing slope – you know, where we used to go look for the first violets in the spring."

"Oh, I remember." Sarah's eyes were soft as she thought of the many times she had gone to that very hill as a girl. And now her children would get to enjoy it as well. "It would be really special to go with all my sisters and my children," she said. "I think it's still a little cool for Esther, though . . ."

"I'm sure Carol and I could watch her for a while," Mom offered. "Why don't you go with them, Sarah?"

A white-throated sparrow was singing as the group made its way down the path. Noah, Judah, and Lydia walked slowly, stopping to look at every bit of green peeking up from the brown earth.

"Mommy, look!" Judah stopped so suddenly that Sarah nearly tripped over him. "See those little furry things?"

"These?" she queried, bending down a branch for a closer look. "These are called pussy willows. They are the flowers of the bushes."

"And look here," Janet added. "See these red things? They're maple flowers."

"They don't look like flowers," Judah announced after careful inspection. "Do you have any pretty ones?"

Rachel laughed. "Come look at these," she called from the other side of the path. "Lydia and I just found the first hepaticas."

Soon it was time to return to the house. The children were laden with flowers, tiny leaves, and pussy willows. Judah even carried a live ant. "Don't you think Grandma will like it?" he asked for the second time.

"She'll probably like it outside better than in the house," Sarah told him, remembering the time years ago when a four-year-old Jeff brought a toad inside. Jeff had, unbeknownst to Mom, tenderly placed the toad beside his shoes under the edge of his bed, just before Mom came into the room to tuck him in. Instead of staying beside Jeff's shoes, it had ended up in the hall, and Mom had nearly stepped on it while going to check on the children that night. Animals of any kind had been taboo in the McLean house since that time.

Reaching the house, they found that Jeff and Jenny had just arrived and were admiring baby Esther. After the children displayed their treasures, they were ready to stay inside for a while and play with the unfamiliar toys. Jenny and Sarah wanted to stay in as well, enjoying the chance to visit. *Jenny fits in so well,* Janet thought. *I'm glad she's part of our family.* God had given her so many wonderful relatives.

"Let's go find the boys," Rachel suggested. "I think they were finishing up some chores, and Steve was hoping we could play volleyball when they were done."

Volleyball was fun with such a big group. They chose sides, and were soon having a spirited game. It wasn't long, however, before Janet was feeling disturbed, and it had to do with Daniel. He was a good player, but he kept putting down those who weren't as skillful, especially his sisters. The girls didn't seem to notice or mind it, and Janet wondered if she was being overly-sensitive. *Maybe they are used to it,* she thought. It bothered her, though. It seemed immature for Daniel to make such a big deal over a poor shot. After all, it was only a game!

Janet stood thinking, completely forgetting that she was in the middle of a volleyball game. She looked up just in time to see the ball sailing toward her. Her fingers barely brushed it as it went over her head, and fell behind her. "Oooooh," her team chorused.

She turned quickly to retrieve the ball, and she heard Steve saying, "Hey Janet, you're playing like me! Better follow someone else's example!"

She smiled at him gratefully as she turned around. Steve loved to make people laugh, but he was careful not to say things that could hurt someone. *I'm glad I'm not on Daniel's team,* she thought. The thought surprised her. Here she had been so excited at the prospect of getting to know him better, and now that she was, she wasn't enjoying it. *Of course I knew he wasn't perfect,* she told herself. Still, it was disappointing to see his faults.

The afternoon passed quickly. Everyone, including the parents and younger children, spent time outside. After an energetic game of freeze tag, the adults sat on the porch and watched the children play. Janet enjoyed a conversation with Mrs. Williams – enjoyed it, that is, until she had the sudden impression that she was being evaluated.

"And your mom says you like to help teach?" Mrs. Williams was saying.

"Well, I . . . yes, I think so. It's a challenge, and I had a hard time at first, but the Lord has taught me a lot through it," she replied. *I hope she doesn't think I said that to impress her!* she thought.

"So what do you think about teaching your own children? Are you ready for that?"

"Well, I don't know. I mean, if God has that for me in the near future, I know He'll help me, but I'm certainly no expert!"

"I'm sure you'll do fine," Mrs. Williams assured her. "You seem like a very capable young lady."

Capable. Janet liked the sound of the word. She wondered why Mrs. Williams was asking all these questions, though. She had the distinct feeling that she was being "checked out," and it made her uneasy.

Evening found Janet even more uneasy. Mr. Williams had engaged her in conversation, and although the topic didn't have anything to do with marriage, she felt that he was weighing her answers carefully. He seemed pleased, however, like Mrs. Williams. Janet couldn't help thinking that this visit had a definite purpose.

But she was seeing more and more little things that bothered her about Daniel. He hadn't offered to help with the dishes, even when Jeff and Luke did. She probably wouldn't even have noticed it, except that she was watching him pretty closely now. Janet was a hard worker, and enjoyed working with her family. To her disappointment, Daniel always seemed to find a way around helping. She was realizing that he was just an ordinary young man, with all the normal strengths and weaknesses common to the human race. Perhaps his faults were different than her brothers', but that was just his personality. *He's still a nice young man,* she thought. *But he's not the wonderful person I had built up in my mind. I guess you don't see all the sides of someone's personality in a few hours.*

The next day she decided that her attraction had only been superficial. The more time she spent with Daniel, the more she realized that she wasn't even attracted to him anymore. He was a nice young man, and certainly had a lot of good points, but she found herself clashing with him, if only in her thoughts. The two families took a walk through the hayfield in the morning, and it seemed that Daniel ended up walking near Janet much of the time. He was friendly and talkative as usual, but she didn't enjoy the conversation like she thought she would. She found herself getting irritated and frustrated, and she wondered why.

I guess it's because I'm disappointed, she thought. *If I hadn't put him on such a pedestal earlier, maybe I wouldn't have been surprised to see that he's just a normal person.* What had she been expecting, anyway? He *was* a nice Christian young man – but for some reason, Janet just couldn't seem to enjoy being around him. *How could I have thought he was someone I would like to possibly marry?* she wondered, shaking her head. He had just told her that he thought a lot of things were too much work, and that he would "rather read about things than do them." There was nothing wrong with that, she admitted to herself, but it certainly didn't appeal to her. She couldn't imagine living with someone who didn't share at least a little of her enthusiasm for new projects.

Besides that, his sense of humor grated on her nerves. *I wish he was a little more like Steve,* she thought, remembering that she had originally thought he was like her brother. She was glad that she had seen what he was really like, though. Now she could stop thinking about him – assuming nothing developed on his end.

That night, Janet again had trouble getting to sleep. She was disturbed about what she had seen in Daniel, but there was also a twinge of remorse over her own failings – the failure to guard her heart. *I might not be feeling so confused and disappointed right now if I hadn't let my thoughts dwell on him,* she realized. *Lord, please help me to keep my mind stayed on You, and just trust You to make Your will clear in Your own timing. Help me to wait, and not try to figure out things You aren't ready for me to know.* She shifted her pillow, trying to get more comfortable on the kitchen floor. *And Lord, help me to be willing to do Your will, whatever it is.*

Janet was more relieved than sad when the visit was over. She had enjoyed the time with her extended family, but the end, especially, had been somewhat wearing. The stress and lack of sleep were catching up to her, and the suspicion that Daniel's parents were watching her overshadowed every conversation. She would have liked to spend a little more time talking to Sarah, but that would have to wait until there were fewer distractions.

The house seemed quiet and empty when everyone left. Rachel and Becky tried to fill the space with chatter about the wonderful time they'd had with the Williams girls, but Janet tried to find work in other parts of the house. She didn't feel like talking about it while her thoughts were in such a jumble. Daniel had turned out to be so different than she had thought. *I'd be able to forget him and move on if I knew everything was over,* she thought. *But it seems like this is the beginning of something more serious. I hope not!*

What would be the outcome of this visit? For several days after the Williams' departure, Janet was on pins and needles, waiting for her parents to call her for a private conference, but time passed, and nothing happened. Maybe she had been wrong after all. A week went by, then another.

Chapter Thirteen

"Janet, can you come here for a few minutes?" Dad's voice drifted down the stairs and into the kitchen where Janet was sweeping the floor.

"Coming, Dad," she replied, taking one more look around the kitchen. It was neat and clean, shining in the afternoon sunlight. Hanging up the broom and whisking off her apron, she headed upstairs.

Mom and Dad were waiting in their room, and they had a chair ready for her. Glancing at their faces, Janet felt her stomach turn over. They were beaming, obviously trying to control their excitement.

No! Janet thought wildly. *Surely not after all this time! Oh, please don't let it be that Daniel has asked to court me!* She took her seat, and her heart plummeted as Dad began to speak.

"Janet, first of all I want to tell you how pleased Mom and I are with your spiritual growth," he said. "We know you aren't perfect, but God has brought you a long way in the past few years. We have seen you surrender more and more of your will and desires to Him, and that has blessed us more than you know. You are a good example to your siblings, as well."

Janet was far from reassured. If anything, her apprehension was increasing. *What else could this be leading up to?* she wondered. She didn't have long to wait.

"Other people have noticed your maturity, too," Dad continued. "And I'm privileged to tell you that Daniel Williams has asked to court you." He paused, smiling, and waited for her response.

Janet sat very still. She couldn't move or speak, paralyzed by conflicting emotions. Her thoughts in those first few seconds were mere fragments of ideas, nothing coherent, but she was conscious of a deep joy that someone had shown an interest in her. Far more overwhelming, however, was the sense that this was all wrong, that this wasn't the way it was meant to be.

Mom leaned forward, looking closely at her daughter. "What is it, Janet?"

"I'm not sure . . . I didn't think . . ." she managed. No wonder Mom was puzzled at her lack of response. After she had told them of her attraction to Daniel, she had every reason to expect Janet to be overjoyed by the news. Janet tried again. "When did he ask?" She didn't want to share her feelings until she had time to untangle them herself.

"He called last week," Dad replied. "They came for a visit because Daniel wanted his parents to observe you and give their counsel."

So I was right about that, she thought.

"Mr. and Mrs. Williams were pleased with what they saw, and after praying about it, they encouraged Daniel to take the next step and call me."

Is this me sitting here, listening to this? I've dreamed of this for years, but somehow this isn't right. After begging God for a husband, how can I be hearing this and wanting to run away? This is impossible! But she heard her own voice, strangely calm, asking, "And I'm sure you and Mom have discussed this and prayed about it?"

"Oh, yes!" Dad returned. He was glad Janet was talking now. Somehow the mood seemed tense, but perhaps he was only imagining things. "We have spent hours talking about it – have you noticed our long walks? We have prayed about it, too, and we felt that God was telling us that Daniel was a good candidate. He and I have had several long phone conversations, and I've asked him a lot of questions about his beliefs. Of course, it helps that we've known their family for years."

"Maybe Janet would like to hear about him," Mom put in. "You've talked to Mark about him, too, and you can share some of that with her."

Dad nodded. "Daniel seems to be a fine, upstanding young man," he began. "He has many good character traits, and really seems to desire to follow the Lord. He also said that he is very committed to being the spiritual leader in his home. He thinks it is important to read the Bible with his family, and 'guide his children in righteousness,' as he put it. I think he is very sincere, and I appreciate that. Many young men don't see that as a high priority."

"That's good," Janet agreed. "Does he want to make most of the other decisions for his family? You know, like we've talked about before, like where to live, or what kind of car to buy."

"I think so," Dad smiled. "We talked about that, and it sounded to me like he would very much be the head of his house."

For the next ten minutes, he outlined the conversations he'd had with Daniel and Mr. Williams, and Janet sat listening quietly, interposing with a question of her own now and then, or nodding in approval. It all felt so unreal. *How can this be happening?* she thought. *And, oh why did my feelings for him have to change? Now what?* She felt a little uncomfortable sitting there, hearing everything about him, when she wasn't at all sure that she wanted to begin a courtship. She also felt a deep respect for his willingness to expose himself like that. *I'm such a private person,* she realized. *That would be almost impossible for me to do unless I knew things would work out.*

"Dad," she surprised herself by saying, "I think you and Mom need to know something."

They both regarded her seriously, loving concern in their eyes. She swallowed the sudden lump in her throat. What wonderful parents!

"I'm not sure what to think about this," she continued. "My feelings for Daniel have changed."

Now it was their turn to sit in silent shock. Without warning, Janet's composure vanished and she covered her face, tears raining down between her fingers. "Why did this happen?" she sobbed, as Mom drew her close. "Why couldn't I go on liking him if it was meant to be? Or why did I have to be attracted to him in the first place?"

"Oh, honey," Mom said sympathetically. She looked helplessly at her husband over Janet's bent head. "Not now,"she mouthed, as he seemed about to speak. She just held her daughter as she wept, waiting until Janet was calmer, and praying for wisdom.

Janet wiped her eyes. "I'm sorry," she said with a shaky attempt at a smile. "I don't mean to question God. I'm just confused and sad."

"He understands," Mom comforted. "He is our loving Father, and He knows our hearts." She paused, then asked quietly, "Do you want to tell us what happened?"

Looking back, Janet was amazed that her parents had been able to understand at all. Her thoughts were far from organized, and she had a great deal of trouble expressing herself, but they were so patient and loving, asking questions to help her sort through her conflicting ideas.

"You know, Janet," Dad said slowly, "I wish you had told us sooner that your feelings had changed. I don't know if this would have – or should have – been prevented, but at least we would have approached it differently. And we certainly could have spared you the last few minutes!"

Janet smiled. "That would have been nice," she admitted. "But would it really have made a difference? I mean, Daniel would have asked anyway. What good would it have done for you and Mom to know about my feelings?"

"Mom and I need to know where your heart is," Dad replied. "You told us when you were struggling with attraction to Daniel, and that was good. But without updates from you, we can't know when things change."

"It's important for us to stay informed, dear," Mom interjected. "That helps us know how we can protect you. And it helps you to be aware of where your emotions are, too."

"I guess you're right," Janet acknowledged. "It's hard for me to come to you and tell you what I'm thinking and feeling. I tend to just keep all that stuff inside. But I can see that I need to overcome that tendency, with the Lord's help."

"That's right," nodded Mom, "Courtship is supposed to be a process that parents are involved in, and we can't do that without knowing your heart."

"We'll try to do a better job, too," Dad said. "We should initiate conversations sometimes, not just wait for you to come to us. It's partly our responsibility to see how you are doing, and I'm sorry we haven't done a better job."

"That's okay," Janet assured them. "What is the next step with Daniel?"

"You can just say no, and I'll tell him," Dad offered.

"Well . . ." Janet hesitated. "I don't want to go on feelings alone, because I've certainly found out they can change quickly! And I know he has prayed about it for a long time. I do think he is a godly young man, and I respect him. The very least I can do is pray and consider it."

Dad nodded approvingly. "I think that is wise," he said. "And you never know – God could change your feelings, too."

The next week saw a serious Janet going about her daily work. She fought to act normally, but the purposed courtship weighed heavily on her mind. Try as she might, she could not escape it even for a short time, and of course she filled many pages of her journal with records of her wrestling.

May 7

It's hard to do normal tasks and go about life as usual with this decision weighing on my mind. Courtship is so serious! I don't want to hurt Daniel by refusing, but since this is "with the intent of marriage," I don't want to let anything start unless I'm pretty sure it will work out. I don't want to give him false hopes.

And yet – how do I know he's not God's choice for me? Could I learn to love him? He is a fine young man, and I truly respect him. Yes, he has faults, but so do I, and if I wait for someone who is perfect, I'll never get married.

May 8

How important are feelings? Daniel fulfils "The List" of what I want in a husband pretty well, character-wise. To be fair to him, he has many excellent traits. He really loves the Lord. He loves children, and I think he'll make a good dad. He's humble – he admitted to Dad that he has a lazy streak (it would be so hard for me to do that!), and he seems to desire to change.

Could I live with his personality? His sense of humor – unlike Steve's – gets on my nerves, and he can be rude when trying to be funny. And he seems a little too laid-back (and maybe irresponsible) from what I've observed and others have said. How much of that could change with age and maturity? Am I willing to take a chance on that? How important are these things, anyway? The heart issues are right – is that good enough?

I have no answers, only questions. I need to share my thoughts, muddled as they are, with Mom and/or Dad. Maybe they can help me see things more clearly. Right now I just don't have peace.

May 9

Dear Lord, give me strength for this! I'm weary of the endless questions. What should my answer be? I had a good talk with Mom today, and she encouraged me greatly. She said that I shouldn't feel guilty about turning him down if he's not the right choice. I do have to remember that if I ever marry, I will marry a real man, not a perfect image I've dreamed up in my mind. And yet . . . as Mom told me today, I should be joyful about my future husband, filled with joy at the thought of being his wife. And, truthfully, the joy is just not there. One thing hit me especially hard – she said, "This is the man you will live with for the rest of your life. You want to look forward to him coming home at night. You want to wake up every morning and say, 'I'm glad this is who I married and no one else.' You want to enjoy his company!" I'm just not sure that would be the case.

But Lord, I just want Your will. I know You can change both of us and make a beautiful marriage out of what looks impossible to me! But is that a wise way to start out?

Despite her continued turmoil, Janet's mind was clearing. The more she thought, prayed, and talked with her parents, the more she realized that Daniel was probably not the right choice. "I don't know how well we would get along," she confided to Mom. "He's a fine young man, but I want someone I would enjoy spending most of my time with."

"That's a very important point," Mom agreed. "You can't have a strong marriage without a strong friendship. Your husband should be your best friend."

Janet forced a smile. "I can't see Daniel ever being my best friend," she confessed. "But really, Mom, it's hard to tell him no! I've never had anyone interested in me before. And apparently he thinks it could work. What if he's right and I'm wrong?" She leaned her head on her hand, weary of the stress but unable to stop thinking. "I don't want to base my decision on feelings, anyway. He has almost all of the character traits I am looking for in a husband . . . and you and Dad approve of him . . ." She stopped miserably.

"Yes, Dad and I approve of his character," Mom nodded. "He isn't perfect, of course, but he is a fine Christian young man. But Janet, if you don't have peace about it, Dad and I don't either!" Mom paused, then continued. "God has one man for you, Janet. There are many young men with all the right qualifications, but of course you can't marry them all! You want the one who is the best match for you in every way – including personality. And Janet," she added, taking her daughter's hand, "If Daniel is the one for you, God will make it clear to *both* of you, not just him."

It was time for a decision. Janet sought the Lord once more in the serene quiet of the woods. "Dear Lord," she prayed, "You know how much I want to do the right thing. If You want me to marry Daniel, I am willing. I trust You to help me love him. But Lord, I think You are telling me that this is not right. I don't fully understand why, but I have asked for direction, and I don't have peace about starting a courtship. So I'm going to tell Dad the answer is no." She stood, turning toward the house, then paused and uttered one last desperate prayer. "Stop me if I'm wrong!"

Chapter Fourteen

May began with an invitation to the wedding of Stephanie Kemp and Micah Haines. *It will be hard to remember that her name is Stephanie Haines,* Janet thought. She wished she could attend the wedding, but she knew a trip to Arkansas was out of the question. "June twenty-ninth," she said aloud, consulting the calendar. "I should have plenty of time to finish her present." She was making a special quilt for her friend, and every stitch was an expression of her love. She had pieced the whole top and started quilting, but there was still quite a bit of work left.

The wedding invitation was beautiful, she thought as she put it on the table for the rest of the family to see. It left her feeling rather forlorn, however. Between her recent courtship-related struggles and the fact that she hadn't heard from Stephanie in three months, it was very easy to feel sorry for herself. She was struck again by the contrast of their lives, and she realized sadly that their relationship wasn't very important to Stephanie anymore.

She was thankful for Anna and Sarah, though. Her friendships with them continued to deepen. At first, she had feared that her relationship with Anna would be damaged as a result of the situation with Daniel, but if Anna knew of the attempt at starting a courtship, she never mentioned it. Janet felt awkward writing her at first, but that soon disappeared. She stuck to less personal topics for a while. She wouldn't be sharing about Daniel with Anna or any of her other friends.

Sarah, on the other hand, was privy to the whole story, and Janet appreciated hearing her perspective. "God has the right man for you," Sarah had written. "Don't settle for anything less! I'm so thankful I waited for Luke. That doesn't mean he has to be perfect, because he won't be, but do wait until you are sure that it is God's best." She also knew a little about the situation with Stephanie. In her characteristic way, she encouraged Janet to love and forgive. "I'm sure she doesn't mean to hurt you," she wrote. "This is new ground for her, and she probably doesn't know how to relate to you. I had a hard time when I was engaged and newly married – I didn't know what to say to my single friends. I didn't want to exaggerate the differences between us, and yet my mind, heart, and life were filled with Luke, and I didn't have much else to write about! That's more than likely the position she finds herself in."

Janet knew all this was true. But she still missed her friend. They had been very close for years, and now Stephanie seemed so distant. *And what am I supposed to do now?* she wondered. *I helped her through her hard times, but now we've drifted so far apart I don't feel I can share things with her like before.*

School let out the second week of May. "I'm at least as happy to be done as Rachel and Becky are," Janet told Mom. "It was certainly good for me, but I'm ready for a break!"

Mom laughed. "So am I," she replied. "I'm always ready to be done in the spring. But every fall, I'm excited about starting again." Janet hoped she would be, too. Right now, she was just glad to be done – glad to have more time to spend outside. Plants were popping up everywhere in the garden, and she worked there most mornings, enjoying the cool breeze and the bird songs. Morning always seemed so peaceful and special to Janet. It was as if God had created the new day, full of promise and joy, just for her.

Dad found her there on one sunny morning. She was thinning the carrots, pulling out some of the tiny sprouts so others would have room to grow. She glanced up with a smile as his shadow fell across the ground. "Coming to inspect?" she asked cheerily. "What a perfectly lovely morning!"

"It is beautiful," Dad agreed, returning the smile. "Janet, would you like to go to Stephanie's wedding?"

The question took her completely off guard, and for a moment she sat in stunned silence. Did Dad mean she could go? "What do you mean?" she asked slowly, finding her voice again.

"Mom and I have decided that you and Ben can go to Arkansas for the wedding if you want to," Dad said. "It would be a long trip, but I know Stephanie is a special friend, and I really want you to be able to go. We can't all leave the farm, but we can spare you and Ben for a week."

"Oh, Dad!" Janet threw her arms around him. "Thank you so much! Does Ben know?" *I can't believe it,* she thought. *I didn't think there was even a possibility I could go! I'll have to call Stephanie and tell her.*

"I'll let you tell Ben," Dad was saying. "I'm sure you two will want to start thinking about your route."

Ben, usually reserved and quiet, was nearly as excited as Janet. "Maybe we can spend the night at Uncle Jim's on the way down," he suggested as they pored over the map together. "It's about half way, I think. I'd like to see Isaac again." It had been several years since he had seen his cousin.

Janet called Stephanie that evening. "Oh, Janet, that's wonderful!" she enthused. "I'm so glad you'll be here. I haven't seen you for so long – and besides, I want you to meet Micah!"

It was good to be talking to Stephanie again. *I've really missed this,* Janet realized as the girls talked and laughed almost like old times. Maybe seeing each other again would help close the gap that had developed between them.

It seemed like only a few days went by, but suddenly it was the middle of June. Janet, with the quilt completed at last, was trying to get everything ready for her first major trip without her family. Rachel and Becky, now fourteen and twelve, would care for the goats in her absence, and she wanted to make sure they were prepared for any contingency.

"Make sure Ginger doesn't get too much grain," she warned for the umpteenth time. "She bloats so easily. And if she does eat too much accidentally, tell Dad right away!"

"We will," Rachel promised. "Don't worry, Janet. We'll take good care of the goats."

Janet sighed. She knew the girls could handle things, but it was hard to relinquish the responsibility even for a short time. *Why do I have such a problem with trust?* she wondered. *If I don't trust God to help the girls take care of the goats, how will I learn to trust Him with bigger things? Oh Lord, help me to let go and trust You.* Recently she had noticed that more and more of her thoughts were turning into prayers. Bringing requests and questions, praises and sorrows to the Throne of grace was becoming more natural every day, and she wondered if that was the meaning of being "instant in prayer."

The last week passed in the blink of an eye. Janet did some extra work for Mom, washing curtains, cleaning doors, and washing windows. On Tuesday evening, she was high on a stepladder cleaning light fixtures when Ben passed her on his way to the barn.

"Can you believe we're leaving in two days?" he queried.

"I'm so excited!" she replied. "It doesn't seem real, does it?"

"It will when we start driving," Ben smiled. He headed out through the kitchen, and Janet heard the tractor start a moment later. He and Steve were going to do some kind of work.

But the tractor stopped abruptly a moment later, and Janet heard shouts and commotion outside. She jerked to attention and hurried to the door to see what was happening. Steve was running to the house, his face white.

"Call 911!" he panted.

"What happened?" she gasped. Something must be terribly wrong. The McLeans had never called an ambulance before. *Lord, don't let anyone have been killed,* was all she could think.

"It's Ben," Steve said, and Janet's heart stood still. "He's okay, I think, but the tractor rolled and crushed his leg, and his back is really hurting. I don't know how serious it is, but he's in a lot of pain."

That was all she needed to know for the present, and she reached for the phone, hands shaking. The voice on the other end was calm. "Van Buren County 911."

Janet quickly told the dispatcher all she could about the accident, and he said an ambulance would arrive soon. "They're about fifteen minutes out, and the First Responders will be there in about five minutes," he informed her. "Go tell the patient to hang in there." She felt a little better, but that only lasted until she got to the scene herself, and saw Ben lying on the ground and nearly unconscious with pain. The tractor had been moved and Mom hovered over her nineteen-year-old son, bathing his forehead with a cool cloth. The whole family had gathered by now, but there was nothing to do except pray and wait for the ambulance to arrive.

"Oh, Ben," Janet said softly. She and Rachel embraced, then stood together quietly, dry-eyed. The suddenness of the accident had left them all stunned.

The rest of the evening passed in a blur, but isolated moments stood out with amazing clarity. The paramedics' gentle hands and professional manner as they rolled Ben onto the stretcher. Mom and Dad getting into the car to follow the ambulance to the hospital. The siren dying away in the distance, and the emptiness of the house when the rest of the family went inside. The way everyone jumped when the phone rang, and crowded around to hear the report from the hospital. Dad's voice breaking as he said, "He'll be okay, but it looks like surgery will be required."

And then, around ten o'clock that night, Dad came home. Mom would stay with Ben overnight, and the surgery would take place the next day. "I guess this cancels your travel plans, Janet," Dad said. "I'm sorry."

She hadn't even thought of it until then, and she fought the tears. It seemed silly to cry over a trip when her brother was in so much pain, but all the emotions and stress of the evening overcame her, and she couldn't help it. Dad understood. "It's okay, Janet," he comforted, giving her a hug, and she knew what he meant. *All things work together for good to them that love God,* she reminded herself. *Even when it doesn't look like it.*

Chapter Fifteen

The rest of the summer was affected by Ben's injury. Healing was slow and painful, but the prognosis for a full recovery was good. Besides the broken leg, he had injured his back, although not severely. He was unable to do any farm work, though, and the whole family missed his help.

"You sure picked a good time for a vacation," Steve grinned. "This is one of the biggest hay crops I can remember!"

"I'm so thankful the accident wasn't any more serious," Mom said fervently.

"So am I," Ben replied, "but it's hard to sit around while everyone else is working."

Janet could sympathize whole heartedly. When she had suffered acute appendicitis several years earlier, she had felt utterly useless. Now she reminded Ben of the advice he had given her. "Take it easy!" she quoted. "You work hard all the time. Maybe this is God's way of telling you to slow down."

He grinned sheepishly. "You're probably right," he admitted. "But it's not easy!"

Not many things in life are easy, Janet reflected later. Would she always struggle with being single? She had decided to stop hoping for marriage and focus on accepting singleness, but it seemed impossible. She couldn't seem to stop longing for a husband. For a few days perhaps, or even a week, she would succeed in putting it out of her mind, or drowning her thoughts with hard work, but something always happened to remind her of what she was missing. Sometimes it was unavoidable, like the times Jeff and Jenny came to visit and brought tiny David with them. He had been born the week after Ben's accident, and Jeff often came to visit his brother, bringing his wife and newborn son. Janet's heart ached as she held him. She had always loved children, especially babies, but now his little hands and soft cheeks stirred up a longing inside her that was different – and painful in its intensity.

Once the reminder of her loneliness had been as simple as a fleeting glimpse through the car window. A man was walking down a shady driveway, his little girl skipping and chasing butterflies behind him. Suddenly she ran up and reached for his hand, and he looked down and smiled. The scene touched something deep in Janet's heart, and it was a long time before she was able to pass that house without her eyes getting misty.

She had to admit she was still waiting on God to bring her a husband. There was nothing wrong with that in itself, but she knew she was spending too much time looking at the future instead of enjoying the present. Other people hardly improved the situation. It seemed everyone she knew was anxious to help her "start her life," and try as she would, she couldn't escape their helpful advice, and being influenced by their attitudes. In October, when the trees brought out their most brilliant finery, a sweet older lady cornered Janet after church.

"How are you doing, dear?" she asked, peering into Janet's face. "What are you doing with your life these days?"

"Well . . ." She wasn't sure how to answer. This week had gone well, and she had convinced herself that she was content with remaining single. "I'm helping at home."

"Still waiting to get married, eh?" Mrs. Ballard's eyes twinkled behind her glasses.

Again Janet was at a loss for words, wincing as she remembered the many times she had said that in the past. What should she say? Some days she felt perfectly content serving her family, milking the goats, and writing letters. Other days she prayed, "Lord, *please* bring me a husband soon!" with an earnestness bordering on desperation. But was it accurate to say she was still waiting to get married? In a sense she was, and yet more and more she was realizing that life had already started. "I'm just trying to serve the Lord where I am," she said finally.

Mrs. Ballard patted her arm. "I know you are, dear. But it won't be long until a young man comes along and sees a treasure!"

"Well, I just want to do whatever God has for me," Janet replied. "And I'll be single if that's what He wants."

"Don't worry about that! You'll get married. Sarah and Jeff did, and it's about time for you. How old are you now?"

"Twenty-three. I'll be twenty-four in December."

"Well, I'm sure it won't be long," Mrs. Ballard repeated, smiling.

Her words, though meant kindly, bothered Janet the rest of the day. Although Mrs. Ballard didn't know it, she had already had a chance – and turned it down. What if no one else came along? Daniel really was a godly young man, and had many of the traits she wanted in a husband. Had she been too hasty? No one would be perfect. Perhaps she should have given him a better chance. Doubts filled her mind, and she was melancholy for a few days. She finally decided to broach the subject to Dad. Maybe he would have some words of advice.

"You prayed about it for a long time," he reminded her. "God doesn't delight in hiding His will from His children! He has promised to give us wisdom if we ask for it, and He keeps His promises. You can rest in that, Janet. I believe God led you to tell Daniel no."

"I thought so, too," Janet said. "But now I wonder if I made a mistake. He does have a lot of good qualities."

"So do all the young men you know," Dad pointed out. "You know, I think it's sort of like parts of a picture that God puts in your heart. You can see good qualities and character traits in many young men, but some have only "pieces" of the whole picture. Maybe Daniel isn't really ready for marriage yet . . . and I think he will be a better match for someone else, anyway. You shouldn't be looking for perfection in a man, because you won't find it, but you should be able to see that "picture" that God has put in your heart – the picture of a man who loves God and desires the same things that you do."

That made sense to Janet. Daniel was a godly young man, but it seemed that there were pieces missing from the "picture."

"Sometimes people end up with unhappy marriages because they aren't willing to wait for the whole picture," Dad continued. "They settle for just a piece because they think they can't be fulfilled without marriage. I think it's because they aren't willing to let the Lord be their portion."

There it was again – "let the Lord be your portion." Sarah had said that last fall, and Janet hadn't quite understood what she meant. She was learning now that it meant to let God fill up her emptiness, to give her joy that didn't depend on whether or not she was married.

"Thank you, Dad." She smiled at him. "I think I understand. Sometimes it's hard to trust, and hard to remember that God led me to this place. I need to work on believing that He has a purpose in all this."

Dad smiled back. "I'm sure God taught you a lot of lessons through the experience with Daniel, too," he said. "Mom and I were just talking about that the other day. In fact, she and I wanted to have a talk with you and share some of our thoughts about the whole situation. I'll see if this is a good time for her," he added, walking toward the door.

Janet waited for Dad's return with mixed emotions. She knew that now was the time to talk about what should have been done differently, and she was ready to share her thoughts. However, she wasn't too excited about confessing her weaknesses through that time. She knew she had been guilty of encouraging her attraction to Daniel, and that she had not been careful enough about guarding her heart.

Mom followed Dad as he returned to the living room. "Are you ready, Janet?" she asked, patting her on the shoulder. She sat down beside Dad on the couch.

Dad cleared his throat. "Mom and I have some things to share with you, but why don't you tell us some of the things you have learned?" he suggested. "Then we can all discuss what we should do differently next time."

"Well, I guess I can start by telling you that I have a lot to learn about guarding my heart!" Janet began. "It sounds easier than it is, and I feel like I really failed with Daniel. Sometimes I tried not to think about him, but there were times, especially at the first part of their visit here, that I didn't do well at all. I let myself think hopeful thoughts, and didn't try very hard to bring myself back to earth. If I'm honest with myself, I can see that there were times that I didn't care if the timing was wrong or not! I got too caught up in enjoying the feeling of being attracted to him, regardless of what I knew I should do."

Mom nodded. "I know what you mean," she commented. "That's true of a lot of other things in life, too. Many times the Lord has shown me that He wants me to give something up, and I just want to keep enjoying it. Sometimes those things, like your attraction for Daniel, aren't wrong in themselves, but it makes it easy for us to get our priorities confused, and we start focusing on what we want, instead of just trying to please the Lord."

"I know that's true," Janet agreed. "But it was hard for me to know exactly what it meant to 'guard my heart.' I mean, how do you do that in a practical sense? I prayed, and tried not to think about him, but are there other steps I can take the next time I'm in a similar situation?"

"Part of this is our fault, Janet." Dad spoke apologetically. "As your parents, we should have taken a more active role in making sure you were doing okay. I guess since you didn't say anything, we assumed you were doing fine, but we should have checked."

"What would you have told me to do?" Janet questioned. "I should have come to you, but I'll admit I really didn't want help!"

Dad smiled understandingly. "It can be hard to want to change," he told her. "Maybe this experience can help you see the importance, though, of having real help from us. I think what we would have told you – and want to tell you now, for next time – is that there are a few things you can do. First of all, you have to be really committed to keeping your heart and mind stayed on the Lord. That's the key, I think. Like Mom said, being attracted to someone isn't sin in itself. But it can be a hindrance to your walk with the Lord if it's not in His timing.

"As far as practical ways of guarding your heart, I think the best thing to do would be limit your contact with that person. I realize that was impossible when the Williams were here, because Daniel and his parents were observing you for a possible courtship, but that's a good rule of thumb. The phone call, for instance . . . you could have politely ended the conversation with Daniel by asking again to speak to Anna."

"But what if you think that this might be the one God has for you?" Janet asked. "I mean, you might be hindering something God wants to have happen."

"God is able to bring people together without our help!" Dad chuckled. "And we aren't discussing how people meet – just how to guard your heart and emotions if you find yourself getting too interested in someone before you know that he is God's choice. If someone is God's choice for you, He will let Mom and I know. Remember that we pray for that, Janet, very, very often."

"Another thing you can do is focus on serving your family," Mom interjected. "You already do that very well, Janet, but sometimes we need to make an extra effort to really focus on what God has called us to do now. When a courtship starts, you will begin to focus on another person, and that's part of God's plan. But until that happens, that energy and time should be directed toward the family and responsibilities you currently have."

Janet nodded thoughtfully. "I guess I thought I was doing well because I wasn't neglecting my work, but I know my heart wasn't in it like it should have been. I was able to go through the motions of serving, with my mind still on Daniel. Being even more dedicated to the daily routine of life would have helped me steer my thoughts in the right direction, I think."

"You know, it takes a lot of discipline," Dad noted. "These things don't solve themselves! But our strength to keep trying comes from the Lord, not ourselves, and He has promised to help us. And don't forget that we are here to help you in the daily battle, Janet. God has given you to us, and we will pray with you as often as you need us – daily, if you need that."

"One thing that probably helped you was the fact that your closest friends are also committed to courtship and purity," Mom suggested. "If you had a lot of peer pressure that encouraged you to dwell on your attraction, or even if your friends just spent a lot of time discussing those kinds of issues, it would be much harder to keep your focus where it should be."

"I'm glad that my closest friends are my family." Janet smiled at Mom. "You and Sarah have been so encouraging to me over the past few years."

Mom smiled back. "I'm glad," she said softly. "The more you make me your best friend and confidant, the more I'll be able to help you."

"So, besides the big issue of guarding your heart, did you learn anything else through the situation with Daniel?" Dad questioned. "I know Mom and I learned again that God's ways aren't our ways!"

"Oh, so did I!" Janet exclaimed. "I never thought things would work out the way they did, but I know God had a plan. And I learned that feelings can change quickly. For years you and Mom have told us that the decision to marry someone can't be based on feelings alone. Now I really know what that means. I'm so glad I prayerfully considered Daniel, instead of just writing him off because I wasn't particularly interested in him." She hesitated, then continued, "I also learned that sometimes there aren't clear-cut answers for things, like the reason I told Daniel no. It was hard to know what to do, because he was a fine young man in many ways. But God made it clear to me that Daniel was not the one. Sometimes I find myself wondering why I couldn't say yes, and I keep coming back to the fact that I didn't have the peace and joy that I should have had. I trust God, and I know He led me."

"That's the most important lesson you can learn, Janet – trusting God. I haven't completely learned it myself yet, and I've been working on it for a long time! But the more things He brings you through, the more you will learn that He is worthy of your trust, and that knowledge will give you more security in life than anything else could. Remember that He wants you to walk in His will, and that if you truly seek His will, He will make it clear to you," Dad summarized. "I'm so glad you shared with us, and I want you to know that Mom and I are still praying for you. We pray for you daily. We love you, Janet, and we want God's best for you, whatever that is."

"Thanks, Dad," Janet replied quietly, brushing away a tear. "And Mom . . . thanks for being my friend."

Two weeks after that conversation, Janet decided to surrender her desire for marriage for good. *This is final,* she told herself. *No more wishing and longing for something God doesn't want me to have right now.* She determined to completely sever herself from hoping for marriage. It was a cold November afternoon, one of the dreariest of the season, but once again she sought the sanctuary of the woods. The faithful, weather-worn old bench was one place she was sure of finding quiet, and over the years she had come to love it. How many prayers had ascended from that spot!

"Dear Lord," she prayed aloud, "I want to give You my desire for marriage. I've fought this for a long time, and I know I need to surrender and give it to You. Please help me to be fulfilled in You, and to truly be content. I'm tired of longing to be married and hoping to meet someone." Janet was crying. At first she had just been saying words, but now she was realizing their impact. "Lord, I give You every part of my heart! With Your help, I want to put the idea of marriage completely out of my mind. Please strengthen me!"

She wanted to surrender so fully that she would never have to deal with the issue again, but it was hard. The tears continued to fall. "I've been waiting for life to start, but now I want to serve You in whatever way You choose. I want to stop thinking about the future, and focusing on things I don't have. I've been wasting time – time that You have given me to be used for Your glory! Help me to serve You faithfully, *whatever* Your will is for me."

Janet felt better when she concluded her prayer. It had been hard, but worth the pain. Now she could forget about the marriage issue and focus on finding out how she should be serving the Lord. *There will still be trials,* she reminded herself. *But everything will be easier now that I'm through with wishing I was married.*

To her great surprise, the very next day she started thinking about marriage again. *Wasn't I sincere?* she wondered. *I certainly think I was! So why am I dealing with this again? Maybe it's just a habit I have to break.*

Winter spent itself slowly that year. Janet helped with the teaching again. It was far easier the second time, and she found herself truly enjoying it. She especially enjoyed seeing her sisters growing up, and helping them explore new ideas. "I hope I'm a good teacher like you someday," Becky said one snowy afternoon. "You are so patient!"

"Patient?" Janet laughed. "I need a lot more patience! You don't know how impatient I get some-times."

"Well, I can't tell," Becky replied, undisturbed. "You must be pretty patient if you don't mind all my questions."

"Thank you, Becky," Janet answered. "I'm trying – I mean, the Lord is helping me. I still have a lot to learn."

It did seem, even to Janet, that little things bothered her less than they used to, and she had much more joy. She couldn't think of anything she had done to help herself become more patient or joyful. *It's all the Lord's doing,* she thought. *And maybe He is slowly taking away my desire for marriage.* Grow-th was a gradual process, she knew. In time, perhaps, she would be fully satisfied without a husband. Until then, she would continue to enjoy the good life God had given her. She was realizing more and more just how blessed she was, with a loving family, a warm house, and most of all, the knowledge that God was directing her steps.

Chapter Sixteen

"Janet! Janet?" Steve's voice rang through the house. "Hey, Janet!"

"Yes?" Janet hurried down the stairs. "What is it?"

"Have you seen the old hammer with the blue handle? Dad needs it, and he thought he'd seen it in the house."

"Oh, yes, I saw it yesterday . . . Let's see." Janet wrinkled her forehead, trying to remember. "I think it's in the kitchen. Want me to get it?" she offered, with a glance at his snow-covered boots.

"That would be great," he replied.

When her brother went back outside, Janet returned to the girls' room. She was trying to record something in her journal that she had learned, but interruptions abounded. *Oh, well,* she thought. *I still know what I wanted to say.* She picked up her pen and began again.

And now, after three – no, four – months of tormenting myself because I thought I was "unfaithful" to my surrender of all the thoughts and emotions pertaining to marriage, I have come to realize that . . . it's more complicated than it looks. Did I really surrender? Yes, I know I did, and my outlook has changed. Now I've moved beyond trying to accept singleness, and climbed a little higher. I'm earnestly trying to find out what God wants me to do at this stage of my life.

But what I expected didn't happen at all. I thought once I "gave everything to God" all my troubles would be over. I wouldn't think about marriage anymore, and I would just be happy to be single forever. Wow, was I wrong there! I think about it all the time, and the longing is still strong. I think I've learned a few things along the way, though.

First of all, even if you truly surrender something, that doesn't mean you never deal with it again. It means that you accept God's will unconditionally – even if that means He chooses <u>*not*</u> *to remove a longing! (Maybe this is my 'thorn in the flesh.')*

Secondly, God may have a reason for you to go through the pain instead of simply removing it. I started thinking seriously about this after I read the verse that says "If we suffer, we shall also reign with Him" (2 Timothy 2: 12). I used to wonder how I would suffer for Christ. I guess I was thinking of things like being imprisoned for my faith, or some other equally "dramatic" persecution. Now I'm realizing that this seemingly endless waiting, the pain and longing and loneliness, is a form of suffering. It may not look very hard to most people, but it is. And I'm learning the same lessons that everyone learns in the school of suffering: that God is always with me, that His strength is made perfect in my weakness, that His grace is sufficient for every situation.

So am I "done" with the desire for marriage? No. Would I trade the lessons I'm learning through this for less pain? No! I know this is the path God has called me to walk, and I accept it. That is the kind of surrender that "works."

Finishing with her journal for the time, she turned to her correspondence. She had a letter from Anna that she needed to answer. Had it been nearly a year since the Williams had visited? It seemed impossible, but it was true. How quickly the time had passed. *And how many things I've learned in that time.* She picked up Anna's letter to read it again before replying.

Dear Janet,

Thank you for my birthday card – I loved it! The front was beautiful, and it reminded me of last summer. Ahhh . . . summer will come again!

The funniest thing happened to me the other day. Remember the picture I sent last fall of our huge woodpile? Well, I went out to get some wood and almost stepped on a dead mouse! Ugh! (Yes, I screamed!) Apparently it belonged to someone, because then I heard this strange explosive noise, sort of a cross between a pop and a squeak. I turned around and there was an absolutely furious weasel. He just glared at me – he was so cute. I decided to come back later for the wood!

To change the subject (slightly!☺), I'd appreciate prayer in the area of trusting God about courtship. Lately it has seemed especially hard to wait for "Prince Charming" to show up! (Don't laugh at my "princess dreams!" I've cherished them for years, and although it might sound silly, I think it's helped me wait.) Do you have any advice for me, as an older girl who has been waiting even longer than I have?

I value your friendship so much! Thanks for always listening to me.

Your friend,

Anna

Janet had been thinking about her reply for over a week. She wanted to share everything God had taught her over the past year, but where could she begin? And how much was Anna ready to hear? *It took a long time for me to understand as much as I have,* she reminded herself. *And there's still so much for me to learn!* All she could do was try to encourage Anna, and point her toward the truths God had taught her.

Dear Anna,

It was so nice to get your letter last week! I really enjoyed the story about the weasel. It reminded me of the time we had a weasel in the chicken house. Samuel came running into the house like a bear was after him! Thankfully, the boys were able to trap it before it got any chickens.

I've been praying for you as the Lord brings you to my mind, which He does quite frequently. The whole courtship-and-marriage issue is something He has really used to refine me. It hasn't been fun, but it is *so* worth the pain and trials! I had to smile at your "princess dreams," but I didn't laugh, because that was my dream from the time I was a little girl (except I always dreamed of a "knight in shining armor" instead of a prince). I want to encourage you to keep trusting the Lord! If He has a "Prince Charming" for you, He will bring him in His timing, dear Princess. ☺

Even more importantly, I urge you to look beyond a husband. The biggest lesson I have learned over the past year is that a husband won't supply all my needs, or make me completely happy and contented. Only God can truly fulfil us. Do you know why? Because "Prince Charming," although he looks perfect from a distance, is only human. A verse in my Bible reading stood out to me in a new way as I pondered this, and I thought I'd share it with you. "It is better to trust in the Lord than to put confidence in princes." (Psalm 118:9) I know this is a unique application of this verse (to say the least!), so lest you think I have taken this out of context, let me add that the entire psalm is about trusting the Lord to deliver us from our enemies. My enemies are the sins that tempt me daily! And only the Lord can save me from those enemies, and give me grace and forgiveness when I fall.

I have come to the conclusion that it's my sins that make me unhappy, not a lack of a husband. Do I still want to get married? Oh, yes! Sometimes I'm so overwhelmed with the desire for a family of my own that I could cry for hours. But God's peace is wonderful! He reminds me that He knows my heart, and that He loves me more than a man ever could. I still hope for marriage, and there are days when I think I can't go on. But by leaning on the Lord, and trusting His strength, I can truly say that I'm learning to trust His plan and be content.

And God is really giving me contentment. I'm learning to take so much joy in the life He has given me – to notice the little blessings all around me, to delight in my loving family and the fun we have together, to truly *enjoy* serving them. My heart is daily becoming more satisfied right where I am . . . and I'm realizing what a good place it is!

Well, that was a long letter! I guess I got rather carried away. This subject is dear to my heart, since it has been such a struggle for me, as well as such an opportunity for growth. I still don't have all the answers, but God shows me more of Himself every day. Hopefully you can get some encouragement from my rambling. Take heart, sister! Life is short – let us live for God's glory!

In the grace of our Lord Jesus,

Janet

Sealing the envelope, she turned it over to write a note on the outside. "Help! Hostage letter inside!" she scribbled. She smiled as she wrote it, knowing that Anna always enjoyed her notes. Then her face grew thoughtful as she remembered that it was a tradition that Stephanie had started years ago. How Janet missed her friend's cheery letters. She told herself yet again that Stephanie was making a lot of adjustments as a newlywed. *Her whole life has changed,* she thought. It still made her sad to think that their relationship had changed so much, but she was able to accept it the way it was.

Will I go through the same thing with Anna? she wondered. *I don't want to pour myself into another friendship if it will fade away like that.* She was glad Anna had asked her advice, and glad she could share things with her, but at the same time she was almost afraid to get too close. The pain had been so real, and she didn't want to repeat that experience.

But what if this is my ministry right now? I prayed that God would use me – what if He wants me to help other girls that are struggling like myself? Janet knew that Anna didn't really have other friends who would encourage her. Maybe this was her calling for now. She would do her best, casting her bread upon the waters, and trust God with the future of their friendship.

And really, I've had a ministry all along, Janet realized. *Serving my family is one thing I know God wants me to do, regardless of other ways He may use me. Even though some people might think it a waste of my single years to simply serve at home, I know that He doesn't think it's a waste!* She smiled at the thought. *Just think of the fulfilling life Mom has. No one could say she doesn't have a "ministry!" And the same is true for me, even if I'm not married. I can still be a good example to my siblings and a blessing to my parents.*

Chapter Seventeen

Snow swished against the living room windows, and the wind whistled around the corner of the house. Although it was the middle of March, a late snowstorm was pushing its way across southern Michigan, and the McLean farm was getting a fresh white blanket. Janet stood by the door, watching for the barn lights to turn off, signaling the boys' return from evening chores.

Dad walked into the room. "Are the boys still out there?" he asked. "They were about done when I came in a little while ago."

"The lights just went off," Janet informed him. "I think I hear someone on the porch now." She opened the door, and Samuel blew in, followed by a rush of cold air and a flurry of snowflakes.

"Brrrr," Mom shivered, joining the group. "What a cold night! A good night to stay inside and do something fun." She looked hopefully at Dad. "Do you have any ideas?"

"Popcorn," Dad replied. "Whatever we do will be more fun with popcorn. Let's see . . . maybe I can think of a few other things we can do, though. Why don't you and I go upstairs and put our heads together? Janet, you can find Rachel and Becky and get the popcorn started. Look out, dear," he added, pulling Mom out of the way just in time. The door opened again and Ben and Steve came in, stamping the snow from their boots.

"Cold evening," Ben said, closing the door. "It feels good in here, though."

"Hey boys," Samuel began enthusiastically. "We're going to have popcorn and do something fun!"

Janet didn't stay to hear more. She was already on her way to find her sisters and get started on the popcorn. Evenings like this were always fun.

"Okay, crew," Dad announced a few minutes later, coming into the kitchen. He raised his voice in order to be heard over the noise of the popping corn. "Mom and I have come up with a few things to do."

"Really? Like what?" Steve asked, interested.

Dad shook his head. "I'll wait until you're through with that," he said, motioning to the popcorn popper. "It's too noisy."

When everyone had their bowls filled, Dad led the way to the living room. "We're going to play games this evening," he told them. "The first thing we thought of was Pit."

A cheer went up. All the McLeans loved the fast-paced trading game. A bell signaled the start of the game, and soon shouts of "One, one, one," and "I need three" filled the room as the players tried to tell each other how many cards they wanted to trade.

"No, no, Janet!" Steve exclaimed, laughing. "I just gave *you* two oat cards! I don't want them back!"

Janet was laughing, too. "Well, I'm not collecting oats, either," she answered. "I'll trade with Dad and see if I can do better!"

Rachel won the first round. "Barley!" she called, holding up the whole set of nine barley cards.

"Whew," Mom laughed, laying down her cards. "I was just two cards short of having a set of wheat."

"What were the two that didn't match?" Dad asked. "I've got one of your wheats."

"They were hay," Mom said.

"Hey! I mean, hay!" Steve jumped up. "That's where my last two hay cards were!"

The cards were quickly shuffled and divided between the players for another game. Dad held up his hand. "Wait a minute, folks," he said. "This time we're going to do something different. Instead of just calling out how many cards you want to trade, try to say it with a British accent."

"How do you do that?" Becky asked, mystified.

"Like this . . . Oh, I say, do you have two? Two cards, anyone, two?" Dad demonstrated. "It's just for fun, so don't worry about doing it perfectly."

The game started amid much laughter. Ben was the best at this form of Pit. "Pardon me, but could you spare three cards?" he questioned, with a perfect British accent. "You can't? Two, then? It's merely a trade."

"Four with tea? With tea and crumpets?" Steve asked Mom politely.

"That would be delightful," she assured him.

"Hast thou three?" Becky piped up. Everyone burst into laughter, and Becky looked surprised. "Isn't that what we're doing?"

"You're saying it in King James English, like the Bible," Dad informed her. "That's okay, though. You're doing fine."

To everyone's surprise, Samuel won the British round. "Pardon me, but I have all the flax," he said, imitating Ben.

"Good for you, Samuel!" Mom exclaimed, smiling at her nine-year-old son.

"Now what are we going to do?" Rachel asked eagerly. "This is fun!"

Dad smiled at Mom. "I thought they'd like it," he said. "Okay, this time we're going to talk like southerners. You know, the way people in places like Georgia talk, like our friends the Fields."

Becky giggled. "I can do that," she said. "I'll just talk like Mrs. Field. 'Honey, do you have two?'"

Steve laughed. "Or better yet, 'Honey child, do you have two?'"

Soon the cards were again distributed. The bell rang, and trading began. The game moved a little slower than normal, because everyone had to think about how they would ask for cards.

"Hey, ya'll, I'm lookin' for three. Anybody got three?"

"No, honey, but I'm gonna have two . . . ya'll need two?" The contrast between the drawling Southern accent and the clipped, precise British accent of the previous game made it even more hilarious.

"Let's take a break from that for a while," Dad suggested after Mom won the round. "I don't want anyone to get discouraged because I keep winning." He winked at Becky.

"Oh, Dad!" she exclaimed. "You haven't won yet."

"But once I start, I might not stop, and you'd have to watch me win for the rest of the night. Besides, Mom suggested that we play Balderdash."

This suggestion was met with great enthusiasm, and everyone hurried to clean up the Pit cards, get out the dictionary, and supply all the players with pens and paper. Dad opened the large book. "Does everyone remember how to play this?" he asked. "I'm going to choose an unusual word from the dictionary, then everyone else will make up a definition for the word. Then I'll read all the definitions, including the real one, and you can all guess which is the real definition of the word. Are you ready?" Everyone nodded. "Okay, the word is elver. E-L-V-E-R."

The room was silent except for the sound of rustling paper and writing pens. Janet sat for a moment before beginning to write, glancing around the cozy room at her family. *We have so much fun together,* she thought. *I'm so thankful for parents who love us and like to do things with us.* She was also thankful that she and her siblings were such good friends. *I can't think of any way I'd rather spend the evening.*

Steve got up and handed his slip of paper to Dad, which reminded her that she'd better get started on her definition. *Hmm . . . elver. That sounds like a foreign word to me.* "Elver – a Norwegian farm house," she wrote, then folded the piece of paper and passed it to Dad. Soon everyone had handed in their slips of paper, and Dad was ready to read the definitions.

"Okay, everyone, listen carefully," he said. He cleared his throat, then began. "'Elver – an old word for gutter.' 'Elver – a shelf for small pails.' 'Elver – a young eel.' 'Elver – a Norwegian farm house.' 'Elver – a part of a horse's harness.' 'Elver – to waver between two options.' 'Elver – the lever on an old elevator.' 'Elver – a girls' name.'" He let the last paper fall to join the pile on his lap. "What do you think? One of those is the correct definition."

Most people looked thoughtful or puzzled. Finally Mom said, "I'll guess 'the lever on an old elevator.'" That started everyone guessing, sometimes more than one at a time.

"Whoa there," Dad chuckled. "I can't write as fast as you can talk. One at a time, please!"

When Dad had recorded all the guesses, he looked up. "Ready for the right definition?" he queried. "It's 'Elver – a young eel.' You get two points, Steve, for guessing the right one, plus you get one point because Mom thought yours was right."

"Do I get points?" Samuel asked. "Ben guessed mine."

"Yes, you get a point for that," Dad told him. "I've got everyone's points recorded. Are you all ready to play again? We'll go around the room in a circle, so it's Rachel's turn to pick a word."

The game continued – a much calmer and quieter game than Pit had been. As Mom remarked, it was a better game to play close to bedtime. "I think Pit is a little too wild and loud right before bed," she said. "Especially as crazy as it always gets when we play."

When each member of the family had taken a turn choosing a word from the dictionary, Dad added up the points. Janet was the winner, much to her surprise. "How did that happen?" she asked. "I was sure you were ahead, Dad."

"I planned on being the loser tonight," he replied, his eyes twinkling. At Samuel's confused look, he added, "Not really, son. That's just the way it worked out."

"Well, I'm sorry you didn't win even one game," Samuel said. "But I guess since you're a grown man, you can be tough, right?"

Dad laughed. "Yes, Samuel, I can be tough. But it really doesn't bother me. I play games with my family because I like to be with you, not because I have to win. Winning is fun, but if you make that the only reason you play games, you won't have much fun."

Samuel nodded. "I think I would have been happy even if I didn't win," he said. "I just like to have fun with you and Mom – and everyone else," he amended, when his siblings laughed. "We have a happy family, don't we, Dad?"

"Yes, we do," Dad agreed. His voice grew serious. "That's something we should never take for granted. So many people in the world have unhappy families, but God has blessed us with close, loving relationships."

"I'm glad He put me in this family," Samuel said.

"And we're all glad you're part of our family, too," Dad returned warmly. "Now let's read the Bible together before bedtime. I think we're ready for the third chapter of Mark tonight."

As Dad read the familiar passage, Janet was thinking. It was the story of the four men who took their crippled friend to Jesus to be healed. She had always thought that those men were very kind friends, but tonight she saw it in a new light. *What if I was crippled?* she thought. *I know I would have someone to carry me to Jesus. My family would be right there, helping me in every way they could . . . just like they do now.* She thought again of the crippled man's friends. *They showed more than just kindness,* she realized. *It was love – the kind of giving, self-sacrificing love our family has for each other. I'm so thankful God has put me in this family.*

Chapter Eighteen

Spring returned to the McLean farm. The birds came back from their winter homes, the apple tree was covered in fragrant white and pink blossoms, and delicate flowers appeared in the fields. The sun arrived earlier each morning, and stayed later every evening, as if trying to give the new growth the best conditions possible. Wide-eyed calves, wobbling on long legs, wandered over the pastures. And in the barn, the old goat, Nutmeg, gave birth to quadruplets.

Janet saw the new life, felt the warm sunshine, smelled the apple blossoms, and spent hours caring for the goat kids. It was all very similar to other springs, but there was a different feeling in her heart. She wasn't sure what it was, but it was definitely there. It wasn't because school was out, because this was the second year she had felt the exhilarating freedom of finishing the task of teaching for the year. It wasn't because of the baby animals – she had seen dozens of new calves and goat kids, although this was the first year for quadruplets.

Was it because she had finally stopped longing for marriage? *No,* she thought, wishing she could say it was. She still wanted to get married, but she was learning – so slowly she could barely see any change – to take up her cross daily, and to bear the weight in God's strength, not her own. *I wish I would learn faster,* she thought. *But what Mom said the other day is true – the hardest lessons to learn take the longest to really sink in.* Dear Mom. She had become such a close friend and confidant. *She really does want to hear my troubles,* Janet thought, smiling a little as she remembered how patient and understanding Mom was. *God gave her to me for a reason. She's always there for me, and I can trust her. Even if she doesn't always understand what I'm trying to say, she loves me and prays for me.* And Janet admitted she usually did understand. "I was your age once," Mom had said a few days ago. "I can still remember how I felt then." Janet was thankful that Mom was willing to share the lessons she had learned.

What is the difference this spring? she wondered again. *Am I doing something differently? Have I turned some big corner?* Janet couldn't remember any great "mountain-top experience." It seemed to her that life was just going on the way it always had. She still had the same goals, the same desires – to love God with all her heart and to serve Him right where she was.

Wait a minute! she thought. *That's not the same goal I've always had.* Even last spring, although truly desiring God's will, she had wanted Him to give her something more – a husband. And while she still wanted to marry just as much as she had before, she now had something she wanted even more. Now her heart's desire was simply to follow the Lord down whatever path He had for her.

That's it, she thought. *That's the difference. Instead of waiting for the Lord to give me the desires of my heart, I've delighted myself in Him, and He has fulfilled His promise. He has changed my desires . . . now I desire Him.*

Janet looked over the green field, stretching away to meet the edge of the sky. *Yes, that is why this spring is different,* she acknowledged. *It's because I am different.*

Janet was at peace.

The End

Acknowledgments

I would like to thank so many people who have helped me on my own journey:

My family – Dad, Mom, Stephen, Katie, Betsy, Ben, Elijah, Daniel, and Andrew. I couldn't ask for a better family! Thanks for putting up with me. I never have to wonder if I'm loved.

Sonja – the most encouraging friend anyone could ask for! Thanks for catching my vision and prodding me toward the goal, and for reading the book in every stage of writing (even those awful 'partial chapters!'). You are precious and I love you so much!

My wonderful friends and sisters in Christ – Sarah R., Natalie, Trina, Kari, Crystal, Hayley, Jacey, Nissa, Glori, Maria, Anna, Abigail, Sarah B., Rachel, the girls this book is dedicated to, and so many others there is not room to mention you all! Thank you for laughing, crying, praying, and sharing with me. You are priceless blessings from the Lord.

Mr. John Sweeney – thank you for encouraging me to let the Lord be my portion. You were the one who suggested the illustration of the young men I have known being "parts of the picture" of my future husband. You may not even remember that conversation, but I've never forgotten it, and it has blessed me tremendously. Thank you!

Castleberry Farms Press

Our primary goal in publishing is to provide wholesome books in a manner that brings honor to our Lord. We believe in setting no evil thing before our eyes (Psalm 101:3) and although there are many outstanding books, we have had trouble finding enough good reading material for our children. Therefore, we feel the Lord has led us to start this family business.

We believe the following: The Bible is the infallible true Word of God. That God is the Creator and Controller of the universe. That Jesus Christ is the only begotten Son of God, was born of the virgin Mary, lived a perfect life, was crucified, buried, rose again, sits at the right hand of God, and makes intercession for the saints. That Jesus Christ is the only Savior and way to the Father. That salvation is based on faith alone, but true faith will produce good works. That the Holy Spirit is given to believers as Guide and Comforter. That the Lord Jesus will return. That man was created to glorify God and enjoy Him forever.

We began writing and publishing in mid-1996 and hope to add more books in the future if the Lord is willing. All books are written by Mr. and Mrs. Castleberry or their adult children.

We would love to hear from you if you have any comments or suggestions. Our address is at the end of this section. Now, we'll tell you a little about our books.

The Courtship Series

These books are written to encourage the active involvement of their parents as young adults seek a mate. The main characters are committed followers of Jesus Christ, and Christian family values are emphasized throughout. The reader will be encouraged to heed parental advice and to live in obedience to the Lord.

Jeff McLean: His Courtship

Follow the story of Jeff McLean as he seeks God's direction for his life. This book is written from a young man's perspective. A discussion of godly traits to seek in young men and women is included as part of the story. Paperback, 1998. ISBN 1-891907-05-0.

The Courtship of Sarah McLean

Sarah McLean is a nineteen-year-old girl who longs to become a wife and mother. The book chronicles a period of two years, in which she has to learn to trust her parents and God fully in their decisions for her future. Paperback, 2nd edition, 1997. ISBN 1-891907-00-X.

Waiting for Her Isaac

Sixteen-year-old Beth Grant is quite happy with her life and has no desire for any changes. But God has many lessons in store before she is ready for courtship. The story of Beth's spiritual journey toward godly womanhood is told along with the story of her courtship. Paperback, 1997. ISBN 1-891907-03-4.

Journey of the Heart

Written by our 23-year-old daughter, Jeannie Castleberry, Journey of the Heart is the long-awaited story of Janet McLean. Janet, now twenty-two years old, has matured and grown in the Lord. She has many longings, struggles, and questions that she must face with the help of the Lord and her parents. Will anyone ever want to court her? How should she handle her desires for a husband and family of her own? When she finds herself attracted to a young man, what should she do? This is an account of a young woman who is still waiting on the Lord. Paperback, 2005. ISBN 1-891907-15-8

New Books in this Series?

See our web site or write to us for our latest titles.

The Farm Mystery Series

Join Jason and Andy as they try to solve the mysterious happenings on the Nelson family's farm. These are books that the whole family will enjoy. In fact, many have used them as read-aloud-to-the-family books. Parents can be assured that there are no murders or other objectionable elements in these books. The boys learn lessons in obedience and responsibility while having lots of fun. There are no worldly situations or language, and no boy-girl relationships. Just happy and wholesome Christian family life, with lots of everyday adventure woven in.

Footprints in the Barn (Book 1)

Who is the man in the green car? What is going on in the hayloft? Is there something wrong with the mailbox? And what's for lunch? The answers to these and many other interesting questions are found in the book Footprints in the Barn. Paperback, 2001. ISBN 1-891907-01-8.

The Mysterious Message (Book 2)

The Great Detective Agency is at it once again, solving mysteries on the Nelson farmstead. Why is there a pile of rocks in the woods? Is someone stealing gas from the mill? How could a railroad disappear? And will Jason and Andy have to eat biscuits without honey? You will have to read this second book in the Farm Mystery Series to find out. Paperback, 1997. ISBN 1-891907-04-2.

Midnight Sky (Book 3)

What is that sound in the woods? Has someone been stealing Dad's tools? Why is a strange dog barking at midnight? And will the Nelsons be able to adopt Russian children? Midnight Sky provides the answers. Paperback, 1998. ISBN 1-891907-06-9.

Who, Me? (Book 4)

Who (or what) has taken Dad's watch and all the other things missing on the Nelson family farm? Should Dad invest in that fantastic money-making opportunity? And who are those new neighbors through the woods? Are they somehow responsible for the Nelsons' troubles? Read Who, Me? for answers to these and other tough questions. Paperback, 2001. ISBN 1-891907-10-7.

Weighty Matters (Book 5)

A thousand nails in a barn? Why is there a mess in the kitchen at midnight? Who is Molly Buford, anyway? Will the boys figure out why there are leeches in a fire truck? And does Dad have to give up blueberry cream pie forever? Weighty matters, to be sure, but not too hard for the Great Detective Agency! Paperback, 2003. ISBN 1-891907-13-1.

Where There's Smoke . . . (Book 6)

Jason and Andy are puzzled again. Does smoke always mean there's a fire? Will that mysterious key unlock something exciting? What could cause such strange clouds? And how does Cathy come up with such hard clues, anyway? You'll have to read Where There's Smoke..., the latest in the Farm Mystery Series, to find out! Paperback, 2004. ISBN 1-891907-14-X.

The History Mystery (Book 7)

Join Jason and Andy as the Nelson family listens to letters from the past. What did Grandfather really see years ago? What does barbed wire have to do with mice? Those mysterious tire tracks near the barn . . . who made them? And how many batches of chicken salad will Mom have to make before they solve the egg mystery? Read The History Mystery to find the answers! Paperback, 2005. ISBN 1-891907-16-6.

Other Books

Call Her Blessed

This book is designed to encourage mothers to consistently, day by day, follow God's will in their role as mothers. Examples are provided of mothers who know how to nurture and strengthen their children's faith in God. Paperback. 1998. ISBN 1-891907-08-5.

The Delivery

Joe Reynolds is a husband and father striving to live a life pleasing to the Lord Jesus Christ. Having been a Christian only seven years, he has many questions and challenges in his life. How does a man working in the world face temptation? How does he raise his family in a Christ-honoring way? This book attempts to Biblically address many of the issues that men face daily, in a manner that will not cause the reader to stumble in his walk with the Lord. The book is written for men (and young men) by a man – we ask men to read it first, before reading it aloud to their families. Paperback, 1999. ISBN 1-891907-09-3.

Our Homestead Story

The humorous and true account of one family's journey toward a more self-sufficient lifestyle with the help of God. Read about their experiences with cows, chickens, horses, sheep, gardening and more. Paperback, 2003. ISBN 1-891907-12-3.

The Choice

Nineteen-year-old Bruce Cohlmann has a choice to make. He can continue to fish for salmon in Alaska, following a four - generation tradition that he knows and loves. But God seems to be opening a different door for him, and Bruce has to make a decision. How can he know what the Lord wants him to do with his life? The Choice, written by our oldest son, Stephen Castleberry, Jr., tells the story of the steps Bruce takes as he tries to determine God's will. Paperback, 2005, ISBN 1-891907-17-4.

For a catalog, order form, information on new titles, prices and shipping charges please contact us:

1) web: www.castleberryfarmspress.com or www.cfpress.com

2) email: info@castleberryfarmspress.com

3) mail: Castleberry Farms Press, P.O. Box 337, Poplar, WI 54864